I glanced at the others in the kitchen doorway, realizing that Ripley wasn't among them. Neither was Mikey, like I said. Along with James, Bobby T, Brynn, and Olivia Gavener, I saw nerdy Hal Sheen, quiet homeschooler Mary Moore, and new-to-the-show Gail Digby.

That meant one other person was missing besides Ripley and Mikey. I couldn't think who it was at first. My brain was still half asleep.

I was still thinking when there was a loud shriek from elsewhere in the house.

Frank and I exchanged a look. "That sounded like it came from one of the girls' bedrooms," he said.

I nodded. "Let's go."

We raced back down the hall. I was in the lead as we burst into the room.

Ripley was standing there in front of the dresser. She was staring into the mirror, a look of horror on her face.

I could see why. Scribbled on her forehead in bloodred letters was the word MURDER.

THE HARDY BOYS

Undercover Brothers®

Available from Simon & Schuster

HARDY BOYS

Undercover Brothers

BOYS

FRANKLIN W. DIXON

#23 House Arrest

Aladdin Paperbacks

New York   London   Toronto   Sydney

This book is a work of fiction. Any references to historical events, real people, or real locales are used fictitiously. Other names, characters, places, and incidents are the product of the author's imagination, and any resemblance to actual events or locales or persons, living or dead, is entirely coincidental.

ALADDIN PAPERBACKS
An imprint of Simon & Schuster Children's Publishing Division
1230 Avenue of the Americas, New York, NY 10020
Copyright © 2008 by Simon & Schuster, Inc.
All rights reserved, including the right of reproduction in whole or in part in any form.
ALADDIN PAPERBACKS , THE HARDY BOYS MYSTERY STORIES, HARDY BOYS UNDERCOVER BROTHERS, and related logo are registered trademarks of Simon & Schuster, Inc.
Designed by Sammy Yuen
The text of this book was set in Aldine 401 BT.
Manufactured in the United States of America
First Aladdin Paperbacks edition July 2008
10 9 8 7 6 5 4 3 2 1
Library of Congress Control Number 2008920165
ISBN-13: 978-1-4169-6171-0
ISBN-10: 1-4169-6171-2

TABLE OF CONTENTS

Night Stalkers

"**D**id you hear that?" Frank hissed under his breath. I nodded. Then I realized he probably couldn't see me. The hallway was pitch black. "Yeah," I whispered. "I think we should—"

"Shhh! Let's go left."

He started creeping that way, staying low to the ground. I followed. It was so dark I could hardly see a thing. Just Frank's back. Not my favorite view. But what are you going to do?

We rounded the corner at the end of the hall. I clutched the big, heavy aluminum flashlight I was holding. It had been the only weapon around to grab when Frank had woken me up a few minutes earlier. I just hoped I'd have the guts to use it if and when the time came.

Up ahead I could see the pale gray outline of a doorway. It led into the mansion's cavernous kitchen.

At that moment the sound came again. Sort of a tiny, scraping noise, so quiet you could hardly catch it.

I tensed. This was it.

Frank heard it too. He crouched there for a moment. Then, in one fluid motion, he sprang up and flipped on the light switch.

The glare was blinding. I blinked furiously, clutching the heavy flashlight in both hands.

"Where is it?" I shouted.

"There!" Frank leaped forward, already swinging the Wiffle bat he was holding.

That's when I spotted it too. The mouse. It skittered away, avoiding Frank's blow. The bat landed on the tile floor with a hollow *thunk*.

"Gotcha!" I cried as the mouse raced toward me on its tiny legs. I lunged forward and swung as hard as I could.

CRACK!

That mouse was fast. I missed too. My hand stung from the recoil of the flashlight hitting the hard tile floor. I tossed my weapon to my other hand and spun around.

Too late. The mouse was running hard. All I

could do was watch helplessly as its little tail disappeared under the refrigerator.

"What's going on out here?" A red-haired girl wrapped in a robe appeared in the doorway—sly, cutthroat Olivia Gavener.

A big dude with a crewcut was right behind her. James Sittenfeld. He was rubbing his eyes and looking irritated.

"Yeah," he said. "What's your damage, dudes? If you want to fight out your differences, have some class. Do it when people *aren't* trying to sleep."

That was rich, coming from him. He was the last one who should be ragging on anyone else for being inconsiderate. You could sum up the dude in two words: Ob Noxious.

"Sorry." Frank tossed down his Wiffle bat. "I was on my way to the bathroom when I heard our little rodent buddy rustling around out here. Joe and I were trying to take him out before he eats any more of our food."

"Did you get him?" James asked. "If you did, Fatso will probably kiss you." He smirked. "In case you haven't noticed, he doesn't like to share his chow."

James thinks he's hilarious. The rest of us pretty much don't. Not that he would ever notice. He's not exactly Mr. Sensitive.

Luckily, Mikey Chan—aka the "Fatso" in question—wasn't among the crowd of seven sleepy teens now crowding the doorway, staring at Frank and me. I wasn't surprised. The kid is a pretty heavy sleeper. I should know. I've been listening to him snore like a buzz saw in the bunk below me for the past week and a half.

"Well, I'm glad you didn't kill it," Brynn Fulghum declared. "So what if it ate a few crumbs? The poor little thing doesn't deserve to die for that."

Ah, Brynn. How to describe her? You could mention her soft blond hair. Her cute upturned nose. Or the way her eyebrows kind of arch up in the middle. But even all that wouldn't begin to cover how awesome she is. Don't get me started, okay?

"Whatever." James yawned, already seeming bored by the whole conversation. "I'm going back to bed."

"Me too," Bobby T mumbled. He looked even sleepier than the others. His blue hair was sticking up on top of his head. Actually, it always does. But usually it's from mousse or something, not bed-head.

Bobby pays a lot of attention to his appearance. That's because he's famous. At least in his own mind. He's a blogger—a pretty successful one, I guess, even though I'd never heard of him before I met him. He even had his blog optioned by Hollywood.

By now you're probably wondering what Frank and I were doing in a mansion with all these people. The answer is, we're undercover agents with ATAC— American Teens Against Crime. That's a group our dad, Fenton Hardy, started after he retired from the NYPD. The idea behind ATAC is that there are lots of places where adults stick out like a sore thumb. Hip-hop concerts. Skateboarding rallies. That kind of thing. The solution: agents who are teenagers themselves. As soon as we heard about it, Frank and I were on board. Our life has been a total rush ever since.

The two of us have ended up in a lot of weird places thanks to ATAC. But our current mission might be the weirdest yet. We were working undercover as contestants on a new reality show called *Deprivation House*.

Well, back up a minute. When we first got the assignment, we didn't know the name of the show. All we knew was that it was an all-teen reality show. When we arrived at this amazing Beverly Hills mansion, we were stoked. I mean, the place is straight out of the movies. Spacious grounds. Private bowling lanes. Plush screening room. Oh, and did I mention the pool? I especially loved the pool.

But we'd barely gotten to enjoy it when the show's host, Veronica Wilmont, announced that most of it was going to be taken away. Not just the real luxuries, either. Over the course of the show, we were going to lose all kinds of stuff, from junk food to cell phones to cable TV.

That sounds bad enough, right? But don't forget, Frank and I were there on a mission. One of the other contestants was Ripley Lansing. In case you've been living under a rock for the past few years, like Frank—

FRANK

Frank here. And give it a rest already, Joe. Should you really be so proud of yourself for knowing all the celebs from *Gossip Tonight*, anyway?

JOE

Butt out, Frank. Point is, Ripley's mother owns a big makeup company, and her dad is the drummer for Tubskull. Ripley herself is mostly famous for wearing expensive clothes and throwing things at photographers. She signed up for the show to do some image repair. But she got a death threat even before the show started, and her family called in ATAC to investigate.

So that's where Frank and I came in. We went

undercover as Ripley's fellow contestants. Only trouble is, once we got here we found out that *all* the contestants—including us—got death threats. Not just Ripley.

I glanced at the others in the kitchen doorway, realizing that Ripley wasn't among them. Neither was Mikey, like I said. Along with James, Bobby T, Brynn, and Olivia Gavener, I saw nerdy Hal Sheen, quiet homeschooler Mary Moore, and new-to-the-show Gail Digby.

That meant one other person was missing besides Ripley and Mikey. I couldn't think who it was at first. My brain was still half asleep.

I was still thinking when there was a loud shriek from elsewhere in the house.

Frank and I exchanged a look. "That sounded like it came from one of the girls' bedrooms," he said.

I nodded. "Let's go."

We raced back down the hall. I was in the lead as we burst into the room.

Ripley was standing there in front of the dresser. She was staring into the mirror, a look of horror on her face.

I could see why. Scribbled on her forehead in bloodred letters was the word MURDER.

Another Round

"**A**re you okay?" Joe rushed to Ripley's side. "What happened?" I added. The others had followed us into the girls' bedroom. When they saw Ripley, there were a bunch of gasps and little cries of surprise.

"Whoa!" Bobby T had seemed a little quiet in the aftermath of Mouse Quest. Quiet for him, at least. Usually he talks nonstop. It's no wonder he started blogging—that way he can get it all out and nobody has to listen unless they want to. "Hold still, everyone," he added, sounding more like his usual self. "I gotta get my camera. This is so going on my blog!"

Ripley didn't seem to hear him. She was still staring

at herself in the mirror. Her ice blue eyes were wide and anxious.

"Oh my God," Brynn moaned. When I glanced at her, she was clinging to the doorway. Her knuckles were white. "I thought we were done with this kind of thing when they caught Mitch."

Joe and I had thought that too. At least for a little while. We'd discovered that one of the production assistants was trying to scare us out of the house because he'd hidden the loot from an old bank robbery there.

"No way," James put in. "Mitch didn't leave that maggoty dead bird in the shower last night. He was long gone by then."

Yeah. No way had that bird flown in and died on its own. Case closed? Not quite. Joe and I might have caught one bad guy. But it seemed there was still another one in the house.

"Are you all right, Ripley?" I realized she still hadn't said anything. "Are you hurt?"

"Who did this?" Olivia demanded. "Ripley, did you write that on yourself? Because I have to tell you, it's not much of a joke."

Ripley rounded on her. "Don't be stupid," she snapped. "Do you really think I'd ruin my favorite Serge Lutens lipstick for some stupid joke? Grow up!"

Then she seemed to catch herself. She took several deep breaths.

"Sorry, Olivia," she said in a more normal tone. "I—I guess I'm just freaked out."

"Whatever." Olivia rolled her eyes. You don't have to be an undercover agent to see that Olivia isn't a Ripley fan.

Just then Bobby T returned. He started snapping pictures with his digital camera. I saw Ripley's jaw tighten for a second. But she didn't say anything. She just turned away and grabbed a tissue.

"Wait!" Bobby protested as she wiped at the sticky red letters. "Let me get a few more angles!"

She didn't respond. Just kept rubbing until all that was left was a sort of maroonish blur.

That was a big step for her. I don't pay much attention to celebrity gossip myself—

 JOE

Joe here. I just have to say: understatement of the year. Dude, you didn't even know who Ripley Lansing *was* before we got this mission!

FRANK

Okay, Joe. Enough. My point was, apparently Ripley is infamous for having meltdowns whenever the paparazzi get in her face. For her, *Deprivation House* wasn't about the money. She had plenty of that already. No, her appearance on the show was meant to be damage control for her out-of-control reputation. Sort of a kinder, gentler Ripley. Otherwise her parents were going to cut her off until she was thirty.

Just then another girl arrived in the doorway. She was yawning.

"What's going on?" she asked.

That was practically headline news. The late arrival's real name was Ann Sommerfeld. But everyone in the house called her Silent Girl. I guess it was her strategy for the game or something. I'd only heard her speak maybe twice in over a week. But I guess curiosity had gotten the best of her now.

Bobby T and Olivia started to explain. But Brynn cut them off.

"This is nuts!" she cried. "Why does this stuff keep happening? I'm starting to think this isn't worth it, million-dollar prize or not!"

Gail Digby nodded. "Girl, I am so with you." Her voice was shaking. "No cable, no AC—that stuff I'm used to. But this is just crazy!"

Nobody answered for a minute. What could we say? She had a point.

I shot a glance up and down the hallway. "Coast is clear," I muttered to Joe.

He reached for the door of the supply closet.

The closet and the bathrooms were the only spots in the house that didn't have cameras in them. That meant those were the only places where Joe and I could talk privately.

See, nobody involved in the show could know who we really were. As far as they knew, we weren't Frank and Joe Hardy of Bayport. We were long-lost brothers Frank Dooley and Joe Carr, separated as babies and adopted by different families. Joe was supposed to be rich. I was supposed to be poor. Naturally, the producers had eaten that story up and made spots for us on the show at the last minute, no tough questions asked.

Even though it was the middle of the night, we had to be careful. The cameras were only allowed to be on a certain number of hours per day. Some kind of union rule because we were all under eighteen. But the producers didn't tell us which hours they decided to film each day.

"Hey," Joe said as soon as he opened the closet door. "What are you doing in there?"

Mikey Chan stared out as us. "Oh, hi," he said, a sheepish grin on his round face. "You scared me. I, uh, was just looking for more toothpaste."

Before we could answer, he scurried off down the hall. Joe stared after him.

"Toothpaste?" he said. "Yeah, right. More like a

case of the midnight munchies. He was probably searching around in case someone missed a bag of chips in the back when they cleaned out the junk food."

"Whatever." I knew Mikey missed junk food more than anyone. He'd made no secret of that. But that wasn't what Joe and I needed to talk about right now. "Come on."

We ducked in and pulled the door shut behind us. "So much for getting away from all the deprivation anytime soon," Joe said. "Looks like we're back in business."

"Right. But we already knew that," I said. "Got any theories?"

He shrugged. "Only that we should have questioned Mitch more before the cops took him away. I mean, we know he killed that other PA to get on the show. But what if it wasn't him behind all the other mischief? We already suspected he might not be the one who sent those threatening notes at the beginning."

"I thought of that too. But it's too late to worry about it now. We had no way of knowing the pranks would continue on without him."

"Okay. So who has a motive to try to freak people out?"

I thought back over our earlier list of suspects.

"Well, there's still Bobby T," I said. "The more juicy stuff he can write up for his blog, the more likely he'll get that movie option picked up again."

"True. And he'd probably love it if he could get Ripley to freak out—talk about breaking news!"

"Yeah. Then there's Ripley herself. We thought she was setting herself up to look like a hero before. Maybe now she's trying to win sympathy as a victim. And James—he's so hypercompetitive that I could see him doing just about anything to win."

Joe grinned. "But do you think he knows how to spell 'murder'?"

I barely heard him. My mind was clicking away, trying to sort stuff into logical order. "Who could have sneaked in and written on Ripley's face while she was asleep? Maybe one of her roommates, or—"

I bit back the rest of my words as the closet door swung open with a whiff of nicotine. A short, wiry woman was standing there. She was wearing a striped bathrobe and looked vaguely familiar—I was pretty sure she was a production assistant.

"What are you two doing in there?" she snapped irritably. "And what's with the racket? Don't you kids ever sleep? You're giving me a migraine! Get back to bed!"

She whirled around and stomped off. "I'm thinking she's not a night person," Joe said.

"Yeah. She's one of the PAs, right?"

"Her name's Sylvia. Brynn told me she's a total spaz. Just about took her head off when Brynn asked her to help her close her bedroom window."

"Guess we should get back to bed like she said." I headed out into the hallway. "Otherwise Veronica will probably be along to yell at us next."

Joe shuddered. "And *nobody* wants that."

"So what do you guys think the next competition will be?" Olivia stirred her cold cereal. All our food was cold—one of the luxuries we'd already lost was hot food. No stove, no microwave, no coffee-maker.

James stopped shoveling his breakfast into his mouth just long enough to answer. "Doesn't matter," he said. "Whatever it is, I'm going to kick all your butts. You might as well take the rest of that quitter's money right now."

That was another rule of the show. Each week, Veronica and a couple of other judges reviewed the footage and decided who was handling the deprivation the worst. That person got kicked out.

You were also allowed to drop out on your own. The first person to do so had received fifty thousand dollars. For the second dropout, the payout had dropped to forty grand. The next three to leave voluntarily would get thirty, twenty, and ten thousand respectively. After that, nada.

Ripley got up and took her dishes to the sink. To get there, she had to step around one of the three cameramen who were filming us at the moment.

"Who's going to chop more wood for the fire?" she asked. "I was freezing last night."

That was our latest deprivation. The morning before, we'd all still been reeling from (a) finding out about Mitch; (b) Veronica introducing Gail as our new surprise housemate; and (c) James finding that rotten old dead bird in the shower.

As if all that wasn't enough, Veronica had announced another new set of deprivations that afternoon. They all had to do with temperature. We'd already lost hot food. Now we were losing extra-cold food too. No more freezer. Also, we were no longer allowed to use the heat or AC in the house.

No biggie, right? Bet you thought the weather is always perfect in Southern California. Yeah, so did I—until we got here. Daytime isn't bad. A little stuffy, but opening the windows helps a lot.

But at night, it's chilly up among all those canyons. Veronica pointed out that we were still welcome to use the huge walk-in fireplace in the great room on the second floor. If we kept a fire going in there, it kept the whole house reasonably warm.

"You got broken arms, princess?" James asked Ripley. "I didn't see you out there splitting wood yesterday. Afraid you'd break a nail?"

Ripley's shiny happy new persona wasn't perfect yet. But even she was getting pretty good at ignoring James's rude comments.

Bobby T let out a yawn, stretching his arms over his head. "I'm kind of hoping there's no competition today," he said. "Ripley's little makeover last night really cut into my beauty sleep."

"I know what you mean." Mary shivered. As usual, the home-schooled girl was so quiet and sort of drab that I'd almost forgotten she was there until she spoke. "Who do you guys think is doing all the scary stuff?"

"Want to know what I think?" Olivia put in. "I think it's the producers."

"Huh?" said Joe.

"Think about it." Olivia looked smug. "They could be trying to spice things up. I mean, it's not like anyone is being killed this time. A dead bird? Lipstick on the face?" She shrugged. "Pretty tame stuff."

"No way." Brynn was sitting across the table from me, between Joe and Silent Girl. She looked tense. "They wouldn't do that. Especially after what happened with that Mitch guy."

Mary nodded. "The stuff that's been going on is too creepy to be planned like that."

"I'm not so sure." This time it was Hal who spoke up. That was kind of a surprise. He usually goes around in his own world. Literally. He's creating a fictional planet called L-62. He's hoping to turn it into a video game when it's finished. That's why he's on the show—to try to win the seed money to produce the game.

"What do you mean?" I asked him. He might be weird, but he's not stupid. And Joe and I learned long ago that it pays to look for clues and ideas wherever we can find them.

Hal shrugged. "This mansion is where that director guy killed his wife right in front of their little daughter, right?" he said calmly. "Maybe the show is hoping to cash in on that. Scare us all to death while we're here. Sounds like good TV, right?"

"Dude!" James looked at him with more respect than he'd shown anyone else in the house so far. "You're totally onto something there! That makes perfect sense."

"No, it doesn't," Gail Digby argued. "This show is supposed to be about deprivation. Showing who can cut it without every little thing they want and who can't."

"Maybe, maybe not," said Olivia thoughtfully. "The whole deprivation thing could be a red herring. Like that show *My Fabulous New Boyfriend,* remember? They told the contestants they were competing for a date with a hunky movie star, but the guy was really just some Hollywood janitor who looked like a troll."

Brynn shook her head. "No way." Her voice shook a little. "They wouldn't do that."

"Don't be stupid," James said. "Who could resist a fun little show about a grisly murder?"

"No!" Brynn stood up suddenly, almost tipping over her glass of OJ. "I don't believe that!"

She turned and raced out of the room. Joe was on his feet immediately. "I'd better go see if she's okay."

"No, I'll do it." I caught up with him halfway to the door.

"I said I'd go," he insisted.

I shook my head. "She needs comfort now." I kept my voice low so the whole group wouldn't hear. "Not someone drooling over her."

He glared at me. But he didn't protest as I pushed past him.

I found Brynn curled up on her bed. As soon as

she sat up and looked at me, I wondered if I'd made a big mistake. Girls—well, they make me kind of nervous. Especially one on one.

Still, I reminded myself that Brynn wasn't just a girl. She was someone who needed help.

"You okay?" I asked. "Do you want to talk or something?"

"Knock-knock. Mind if I come in?" It was Chuck, one of the cameramen from the kitchen. He'd just followed me in. It was pretty obvious he was hoping to get some footage of Brynn's breakdown.

"Not right now, man," I said.

He shrugged, keeping the camera focused on Brynn. "Just doing my job, buddy."

"Well, do it later. Right now we need a little privacy." I made my voice firmer this time.

Chuck got the message. He frowned and looked like he was going to argue. But finally he just shrugged again and left.

"Thanks," Brynn said with a sigh when he was gone. "I really don't want everyone back home in Indiana seeing me like this."

"I hear you." I sat down on the edge of the bed. "You okay?" I asked again.

"Sort of." She smiled wanly. "I'm just not used to this sort of thing. I mean, murder, vandalism, arson . . ."

"Arson?" I blinked, wondering if I'd missed something. "What arson?"

"Didn't you hear? Olivia was talking to the new girl, Gail. She said her father went to jail for arson when Gail was just a kid."

"Whoa." I'd already known Gail had had a tough life. Veronica had made a point of telling us all about how Gail had grown up dirt poor, gone to school hungry, stuff like that. But she hadn't said anything about arson. It probably didn't mean anything, but I filed it away in my mind just in case.

Brynn grabbed a tissue from the bedside table and dabbed at her eyes. They looked even bigger and greener when they were watery. I realized this was the closest I'd ever been to her. Strangely, that didn't freak me out too much. It was actually sort of . . . nice. I could see why Joe liked her so much. Although come to think of it, Joe likes just about anything in a skirt.

"Anyway, I guess I've led a pretty sheltered life," said Brynn. "It all just got to me back there. I'll be okay in a second." She smiled at me. One of her top teeth was a little crooked. Somehow, that made her smile seem totally perfect. "Will you sit here with me for a few minutes until I'm ready to go back?"

I nodded. To be honest, I probably would have nodded if she'd asked me to go jump off the edge of one of the canyons out on the mansion's grounds. Don't ask me why. That was just how I felt right then.

"Sure," I promised. "I'm here for you."

Must-See TV

Okay, I admit it. I was distracted every second that Frank and Brynn were off together. Can you blame me? I mean, for the first time a girl had actually realized on her own that I was the hotter, more happening Hardy. Brynn and I were really getting tight, and I was liking it. And now Frank was trying to elbow in?

Well, maybe not. Frank is a guy of many talents, but scamming girls totally *isn't* one of them. He was probably just being sincere. That's kind of his thing.

Still, I couldn't think about much of anything else until the two of them came back. Brynn looked a little calmer by then.

Meanwhile the rest of the group was talking about the old murder. See, that's another thing about the *Deprivation House* mansion. The place even has its own scandalous history. Ten years ago it was the home of up-and-coming starlet Katrina Decter and her husband and four-year-old daughter. But one night the husband killed her, right in front of their kid. Self-defense—that's what they decided at the trial.

"I blogged about the murder when Veronica first told us about it," Bobby T was saying. "I've done some research since then too." He leaned forward, almost putting his elbow into Mary's cereal bowl. "Did you know the murder weapon was a fireplace poker? He used it to stab her."

Ripley wrinkled her nose. "Gross."

"Yeah," Gail added. "Some of us are trying to eat here, you know."

"Fine." Bobby reached for his laptop. He carried that thing with him everywhere. It was like his security blanket. "Then you probably don't want to see the gruesome old crime scene photos I found online."

"No, thank you," said Gail primly.

But Ripley didn't say anything. She just watched with interest as Bobby flipped open the computer.

As for James, he looked downright excited. "Let's

check it out, dude," he said. "Is there blood?"

"Tons," said Bobby. "Just let me pull up the site. . . ."

"Oh my God," Brynn exclaimed. "You know, I think I just lost my appetite." She whirled and ran back out of the room.

Frank bit his lip and stared after her. For a second I thought he might go after her again.

But he didn't. He had to be just as curious as I was to see what Bobby had uncovered. Even though we were in the mansion on a totally different case, it was hard not to be curious about the old murder. Especially one that sounded so weird and creepy.

"It's loading—give it a sec," Bobby said.

Gail shook her head. "I can't believe you're all so freaking fascinated with this," she said. "In my neighborhood, people get murdered all the time. Do you think anyone cares?" She snorted. "Not hardly. Not when it's poor people getting their heads bashed in."

James rolled his eyes. "Give it a rest, Debbie Downer."

"It sounds like such a sad thing, doesn't it?" said Mary softly. Whenever she spoke, she sounded like she was afraid no one would want to listen. "Just imagine how that little girl must have felt watching her father kill her mother in cold blood."

"But it wasn't in cold blood," Olivia argued. "Don't you remember what Veronica told us? Katrina Decter was supposed to be possessed by a demon or something. It made her attack her daughter, and that's why the father killed her. He was just protecting little Anna."

Mary shrugged. "It's still sad. That's all I'm saying."

Bobby glanced up from the screen. "I read that when the cops came in, the little girl was all covered in blood from hugging her mother's body."

"Ew! Are the pictures up yet?" Mikey stood up for a better look at the laptop screen. "Hey, check it out. The page is called Witness to Evil."

"Awesome," said James. "So they *did* teach you to read at fat camp."

"Witness to Evil." Hal looked up from his notebook for the first time. He spends most of his time sketching out every little detail of his new planet there. I swear, the guy probably has lists of every brand of toilet paper sold on L-62. "Cool title. I might use that in my game."

"Somebody already used it," Mikey said. "It's the title of this old made-for-TV movie about the Decter murder. I just saw it in the TV listings—it's on later this week."

"Really?" said Frank. "That's a coincidence."

"Probably not," I pointed out. "The news is out that this show is being shot at the site of the Decter murder. The network probably pulled it out to cash in on public interest."

By now the photos were mostly loaded on the laptop. I stepped over for a look. Frank, James, Mikey, and Silent Girl were looking too.

I was distracted for a second when Brynn came back in. Her eyes were red and puffy. Somehow, though, she made it work. She pretty much always looks awesome.

Then I tore my gaze away and looked down at the computer. I've seen a lot of intense stuff since signing on with ATAC. But I have to tell you, those pictures were pretty grisly. Blood everywhere. They must have repainted the great room since then.

"Whoa," Frank said. "I can't believe these photos are out there for everyone on the Internet to see."

"*Everything* is on the Net these days," said Bobby. "Accessibility is the new privacy." He glanced around the table. "Anyone else want to see?"

"I don't want to see the gross photos, but I wouldn't mind seeing that *Witness to Evil* movie," Olivia said. "It might be kind of cool to watch it while we're sitting right there in the room where the actual murder happened."

"Well, *I* don't want to see the photos *or* that

movie," Gail declared. "Good thing they already took away cable TV."

"It's not on cable," Mikey said. "Regular network. Eight to ten p.m."

I wasn't at all surprised that Mikey knew that. He loved TV almost as much as he loved junk food. And the producers hadn't just cut us off from cable. They'd also limited us to a single black-and-white TV set in the great room. We were allowed to have it on only between eight and ten at night. That meant we all had to agree on what shows to watch. So Mikey spent tons of time poring over the listings online. That way we usually just left it up to him what to choose.

"Dude." James smacked his hand on the table so hard that everyone's dishes jumped. "We are *so* watching that movie!"

"Speak for yourself," Gail said. "No way do I want to watch something like that."

"Me either," agreed Ripley. "I have less than zero interest in that sort of trash TV."

"Obviously." James smirked at her. "That's totally why you agreed to play a corpse in *Forest of Blood Four*. That one was pure class."

Ripley glared at him for a second. Then she turned away and suddenly got very busy adding milk to her cereal.

"So?" Mikey said. "Should we take a vote on whether to watch *Witness to Evil*?"

"You can put me down for no." Gail's face and voice were stony. "I'm not watching a bunch of rich people kill each other."

Nobody else got a chance to vote. That was because Veronica Wilmont strode into the kitchen at that moment.

"Good morning, people," she said in her icy voice.

I don't usually notice stuff like fashion. But Veronica's outfits are pretty hard to miss. Today she was wearing a tight purple suit with a very short skirt and matching purple spike heels. Her white-blond hair was flawless, as always.

"I hope you all slept well," she went on. As usual, she didn't sound like she cared much one way or the other. "And you might want to get a good night's sleep tonight, too. Because your next competition will take place bright and early tomorrow morning." Her smile slid into a smirk. "And I do mean *early*."

She spun on her heel and left. We all spent the rest of the meal speculating on what that might mean. After that, it was Frank's turn to help do the breakfast dishes. Meanwhile I took advantage of the free morning to do some laundry. ATAC hadn't warned me to bring more than a week's worth of underwear.

Frank came and found me when he was finished with his chores. All he said was "Want to take a walk?" But I knew he really wanted to talk about the mission.

We tried the bathrooms, but they were both occupied. Next we headed for the supply closet. But that spastic PA, Sylvia, was digging around in there. I guess she was having trouble finding whatever she was looking for, because she was cursing like a sailor and muttering something about needing a cigarette. I don't think she even noticed us.

"Let's go outside," Frank suggested.

We still weren't sure how many cameras were set up outside. But the grounds were so vast, it seemed impossible they could cover the whole place.

Just outside the back door, we found James lifting weights on the grass near the covered-over pool. At first I wondered why, since there was an awesome state-of-the-art exercise room in the mansion's basement.

Then I saw Ripley and Brynn. They were lying on a couple of teak lounge chairs, dressed in bikinis. Nice.

"Sure you don't want to take a turn, fatso?" James taunted as he lifted.

I hadn't even noticed that Mikey was out there too. Can you blame me?

Ripley lowered her designer shades and peered at James. "If you want to work up a sweat, why don't you chop more wood?" She gestured at the pile of split logs at the far end of the grassy part of the yard. "We're all going to be cold tonight if we don't keep the fire going."

"Ugh. Hard to believe. It's boiling out here now." Mikey squinted up toward the sun, then took a swig out of the glass of ice water he was holding.

I was surprised to see that ice water. No freezer meant no ice maker, either. Veronica had explained that if we wanted ice, we had to get it the old-fashioned way. There was a big block of it in a shed behind the woodpile. We were welcome to chip pieces off and haul them back to the house.

James looked surprised too. "Hey, where'd you get that ice water, Chubby Chan?"

Mikey shrugged. "There's a pitcher in the fridge." He took another sip and grimaced. "Yuck. I hate water. I wish they hadn't taken our soda away."

"You should be thanking them." James swung the weights up over his head. "There are no calories in water."

"Whatever," Mikey muttered.

I rolled my eyes. Sure, Mikey could stand to lose

a few pounds. Okay, make that a few dozen. That didn't give James the right to razz him nonstop.

"What'd you say, chubby?" James asked. "I couldn't quite hear you. Your blubber must be soaking up the sound waves from your voice."

"Hey, James. Lay off already, okay?" Frank's voice was mild, but I know him pretty well. I could tell he was getting steamed.

"Yeah," I backed him up. "Enough, dude."

James shot us an irritated look. "I don't like people telling me what to do," he said. "That's not a threat—it's a fact."

"Grow up, James," Brynn put in. "You may think you're funny, but you're not."

Mikey didn't say a word. He was staring into his glass, looking embarrassed and kind of sad. I felt bad for him. He seemed like a nice guy.

Ripley wasn't saying anything either. She was just lying there watching us. Sort of like we were some slightly boring TV show.

James dropped his weights on the grass. "Fine," he said. "I was just about to hit the shower anyway." He strode across the lawn.

When he reached Mikey's lounge chair, he stopped. Mikey stared up at him, looking nervous.

James's hand shot out. Mikey cringed, obviously thinking he was about to be hit.

I thought so, too. My muscles tensed automatically, ready to jump in. Beside me, I could sense Frank reacting the same way.

But James only grabbed Mikey's glass. He chugged the water and most of the ice. "Thanks, dude," he said, chewing the ice cubes as he talked. "I needed that."

He grinned, then spit a small chunk of ice in Mikey's direction. It bounced off Mikey's head. Brynn gasped in shock.

"Listen, fatty," James said, tossing the glass back to Mikey, "I had to chip that ice myself. From now on, keep your meaty little paws off it, okay?"

Ripley stood up and stretched. "Am *I* allowed to have any of your precious ice?" she asked. "I'm hot."

"Yes, you certainly are." I was surprised James wasn't actually drooling as he took in the sight of her in her bikini. "Come on, ice princess. I'll pour you a glass myself."

Hot or Cold

After James and Ripley left, Joe and I hung out with Brynn and Mikey for a while. We chatted about the show, the next challenge, and of course, the strange happenings lately.

"What do you guys think of Olivia's theory?" Joe asked at one point. "You know—about how maybe the producers are doing freaky stuff like planting that dead bird in the shower just to mess with us."

I knew he was feeling the others out, trying to make them say something to give themselves away. That was one of the first things we learned in our ATAC training—get whatever info you can out of the locals without letting them know that's what you're doing.

Then again, maybe Joe was just making small talk with Brynn. After all, she and Mikey weren't exactly our prime suspects.

"I don't know." Mikey shot a slightly nervous glance at the house. He seemed kind of distracted. Was he afraid James might come back for more? "Maybe."

"I hope it's not true," Brynn said. "The show doesn't need it."

"What do you mean?" I asked.

She shrugged. "I mean it's interesting enough just finding out what it's possible to live without. There's some stuff you take for granted—stuff you really don't notice much until it's gone. You know, like cell phones. Or ice."

Mikey frowned. "Yeah," he muttered. "You don't notice it except when James is chewing on it all the time. Totally gross."

I raised an eyebrow. Working for ATAC, you learn to be pretty observant. But I had to admit, I hadn't noticed James's ice-chewing habit before this. Then again, James had mostly left me alone. It was no wonder if Mikey was a little more sensitive.

The door opened and Veronica stepped out. She looked even more purple in the sunlight. Like a giant eggplant, only skinnier and with blond hair.

"Interesting," she said. "Given that it's supposed to drop into the forties tonight, I would have thought you'd be working a little harder at chopping wood for the fire."

"How are we supposed to know the five-day forecast?" Joe murmured. "The Weather Channel's on cable."

Veronica shot him a look. I wasn't sure if she'd heard him or not. "See you tomorrow morning at the competition," she said, then spun on her heel and disappeared back into the house.

I stood up. "Come on," I said to Joe. "I'll split if you stack."

Chopping firewood is hard work. But I didn't mind. The physical labor gave me time to think. One of the things I thought about was our host, Veronica Wilmont. So far Joe and I hadn't seriously considered her a suspect. Was that a mistake? She certainly had enough access to do just about anything she wanted. And she seemed mean enough to pull the most recent pranks. But what could be her motive? Could Olivia's theory be right? Or could Veronica possibly be doing it on her own?

SUSPECT PROFILE

Name: Veronica Wilmont

Hometown: Los Angeles, California, by way of Minnesota

Physical description: 5'11", 130 lbs., white-blond hair, green eyes.

Occupation: Reality show host

Background: Came to Hollywood ten years ago as an aspiring actress. Played bit parts in minor films and on TV before landing lead role in failed sitcom. After that, worked odd jobs before getting hired as fill-in host for a couple of game shows, which led to the job on _Deprivation House._

Suspicious behavior: Her job description—lurking around and watching us. She knows everything that goes on in this house and never lets us forget it.

Suspected of: Staging nasty pranks to freak us out, maybe to take advantage of our leftover fear from Mitch's crimes.

Possible motive: Wants to make sure the show is a ratings success. It could make her career and ensure that she never has to play Stabbing Victim Number Four again.

● ● ●

"Ms. Wilmont, I need you to come to the Depriva-tion Chamber with me." Sylvia, the skinny, hyper little production assistant, bustled into the kitchen that night. "They want you to do some more on-camera commentary before tomorrow's competi-tion."

"Right now?" Veronica snapped. "Can't it wait?"

Sylvia rolled her eyes. "Look, the director said to go get you, so here I am. Are you coming or not?"

"Fine." Veronica scowled at her, though Sylvia didn't seem to notice. The PA was already racing back out of the room like a monkey hopped up on caffeine.

Veronica glanced around the kitchen. Most of the contestants were still gathered around the table. Only Hal and James were missing.

"I suppose this is good night, then," she told us. "I'll see you in the morning for the competition."

"Man, finally!" Bobby T burst out as soon as she was gone. "I thought she was going to hang around all night."

"Me too." Joe grinned. "Guess she likes our com-pany."

Olivia looked smug. "That's not why," she said. "A little bird told me they turned off the hidden cameras at five p.m. today. Veronica was probably just sticking around to observe us like she warned she'd be doing."

"A little bird?" Ripley echoed.

I was wondering about that too. We weren't supposed to know when the cameras were on or off. Veronica had even mentioned once that the camera guys would sometimes wander around and pretend to film us even after hours, just to keep us on our toes.

Even so, we kind of figured everything was mostly off at night when we were all asleep. Watching Joe drool or listening to Mikey snore wouldn't exactly be a ratings grabber. And of course, we knew we were on camera during the competitions and whenever someone quit or got kicked off the show. As for the rest of the time, it was anybody's guess.

After a little more questioning, we got Olivia to admit where she'd gotten the scoop. The camera guy Chuck had let it slip earlier that day. Since the next day's competition was starting earlier than usual, they were shutting down filming early today to make up the time.

It was just as well. Not much had happened that day. It's kind of amazing how much down time there is on reality shows. No wonder they can squeeze a whole week into one hour.

Bobby T kicked back and put his feet up on the kitchen table. Veronica hates that.

"Ol' Ronnie seemed kind of pissed off at that skinny chick, didn't she?" he commented.

"Big surprise. She seems pissed off by everyone," said Mikey.

"So what do you guys think they have in store for us tomorrow morning?" Gail wondered. "All Veronica said was that we'd be starting early."

"Ugh," Bobby groaned. "Guess that means I'm not going to win. I'm useless until, like, noon. So whoever *does* win—do me a solid and don't get rid of Internet service, okay?"

"Or TV!" Mikey added quickly. "We only have two hours as it is."

"I'm with you there," Olivia agreed. "I definitely don't want to lose our TV before we see that movie about the Decter murder."

"Neither do I," Mary admitted. Silent Girl nodded. I guess we were all curious about that old murder.

Brynn got up and walked to the refrigerator. "Anyone want anything?" she asked. "I'm going to have a glass of water."

"No thanks." Ripley glanced over at the wall near the door.

A list of potential deprivations was posted there.

Several were already crossed out. iPods. Hot food. Phones. Extra bathrooms. Cable. Junk food. Freezer. Heat and AC. But there were still plenty more to go.

"My vote goes to keep makeup and toiletries," said Ripley as she scanned the list. "I don't think anyone is going to want to see what we'll all look like on TV without shampoo or concealer, right?"

"Ugh, good point." For once, Olivia seemed to be in total agreement with Ripley. She smoothed down her wavy red hair. "Without conditioner and gel, my hair will totally frizz. I'll look like Little Orphan Annie."

Just then James strode into the room. Judging by the sweaty shorts and tank he was wearing, he'd been working out. That, taunting Mikey, and bragging about how he was going to win seemed to be his only hobbies.

"What are you girls gabbing about?" he asked. "Trying to convince Chubby Chan to sit on me to keep me from walking all over you at the challenge tomorrow?"

I shot a look at Joe. He rolled his eyes. Obviously telling him off that morning hadn't stuck.

When nobody answered, James just shrugged. Then he noticed Brynn pouring herself a glass of ice water.

"Hey, babe, thanks. How'd you know I needed to rehydrate?" He grabbed the glass out of her hand and took a drink.

"Hey!" Brynn protested.

"Dude, have some class," added Joe.

James just grinned and started chomping on the ice in his mouth. But a second later his grin faded. The half-full glass slipped from his hand and shattered on the floor.

"What the—," he blurted out.

As he spoke, the water and ice he'd just drunk spurted out in all directions. Only now it was tinted bright red. James rushed over to the sink and spat the rest of it out. His mouth was dripping with blood!

Going Hungry

"**O**h my God!" Gail shrieked.

I was already on my feet. Frank and I reached James at the same time.

"What happened?" Frank demanded. "What's wrong?"

"The ice." James sounded odd and mumbly as he twisted his mouth around. More blood spurted with every word. "It, like—it cut me or something!"

"Open up," I ordered him. "Let me see."

For once he obeyed without arguing or making an obnoxious comment. The inside of his mouth looked like raw hamburger. Blood was oozing everywhere. His teeth were coated in it.

"It's glass," said Frank grimly. He was bent over

the sink, examining the grossness. Then he squatted down to examine the ice rapidly melting all over the kitchen floor. "Here's more of it. Too much to be just from the broken glass. Someone must have frozen shards of it into the ice cubes."

"But that's crazy!" Olivia protested. "Who would do something like that?"

Brynn's face was pale. "Maybe the same kind of person who would plant a bomb on a lawn mower."

I felt a pang of sympathy. Brynn had had a close call in one of the earlier challenges, when a bomb had been rigged to go off when someone turned on the ignition on a riding mower. The look in her eyes and the quiver in her voice made me want to take her away somewhere safe and make it all better for her. Unfortunately, there was no time for that right now.

"But that bomb thing was Mitch, right? He's long gone." Mary looked pale too. Then again, she always looks kind of pale. She's practically see-through. "That ice water has only been in the fridge since this morning."

"We'd better call the paramedics." Frank was already reaching for the intercom button on the wall nearby.

"No! Wait," said James. He closed his mouth

and sort of wriggled his tongue around. Then he winced, opened up, and pulled out another chunk of bloody glass. "I'm okay."

"Dude, you sure don't *look* okay," Bobby T commented.

Talk about an understatement. Blood was dripping down his chin onto his white tank top. He could have starred in a workout video for vampires.

"If you swallowed some glass, it could kill you," Frank said.

"I didn't swallow any," James insisted. "I just swished the water around in my mouth and then started chewing. Nothing went down—I'm sure of it."

"But why don't you want to go get checked out?" exclaimed Brynn. "Better safe than sorry."

James swiped at the blood on his chin. "No way," he said. "Like Dooley said, I coulda been killed. And the producers are already skittish after all the stuff that's happened. If they hear about this, they'll shut the show down for sure."

"He's right," Gail agreed. "We can't risk it. *Some* of us need that million-dollar prize." She shot a slightly sour look at Ripley.

Ripley didn't seem to notice. "Well, let's make sure there's nothing still stuck in there. Hang on, I'll get some tweezers." She hurried out of the room.

"She's really getting into her role as little miss Florence Nightinheiress, isn't she?" Bobby T commented.

Ripley returned while a few of the others were still giggling at that. But she paid no attention to anyone but James.

"Open wide and hold still," she said. "Is there a flashlight around? That would help."

She got busy picking the remaining shards out of James's cheeks and tongue. It was pretty gross. I have to give her credit, she really kept her cool. So did James. I saw his eyes water a few times, but he let her do her thing without complaining.

"I think I got it all," Ripley said at last. "But you should probably still get checked out by the pros. Maybe you can come up with a cover story."

James spit a gob of blood into the sink. "Yeah," he agreed. "I'll come up with something." He grinned weakly. "It's not like I've never done something stupid and injured myself before. I'm sure I can make it believable."

A few minutes later, he was explaining to Veronica how he'd tried to fit a whole water glass into his mouth and accidentally broken it in there. She looked disgusted, both at his story and the mess in the kitchen. We'd already gotten rid of the rest of the glassy ice, of course, but blood and bits of the shattered water glass were still everywhere. Stepping over to the intercom, she called for help.

Sylvia was the first to arrive. "What is it now?" she complained. "I have a stinking migraine, and I was just getting ready to go to bed."

"Take Mr. Sittenfeld to see the medics," Veronica ordered her. Then she glanced around at the rest of us. "Everyone else get to bed. You have a long day tomorrow."

After she left, some of the contestants did as she said. Others hung around in the kitchen, wiping up the mess and chatting about what had happened. Frank and I ducked outside for a quick discussion.

"This is getting serious again," Frank said. "This wasn't just a prank, like the bird thing or the lipstick thing. James really could have been killed."

"No kidding." I shook my head. "Would Bobby go this far just for a juicy blog entry? And what about Ripley? She could still be pushing the do-gooder thing. Showing she's a nice person by picking glass out of someone's face." I shuddered, realizing that "someone" had almost been Brynn. The glass of ice water had been in her hand before James had snatched it away.

Frank seemed to be thinking the same thing. "Was someone just out to cause trouble in general by putting glass in the ice?" he mused. "Or was James targeted specifically? Everyone knows he's always chugging ice water."

"And chewing up the ice," I added, seeing what he was driving at. "At least according to . . ."

"Mikey Chan," Frank finished grimly. "I guess he's the obvious suspect for this one, isn't he?"

"Kinda hard to believe," I said. "The kid seems so, like, mild-mannered and gentle."

"Yeah. But also maybe a little sneaky. Or at least private. We've caught him a couple of times now skulking around in the supply closet, remember?"

"Still seems kind of weak, if you ask me."

Frank shrugged. "Maybe. But we can't rule anybody out. For now, let's sleep on it—we're getting up early tomorrow, remember?"

SUSPECT PROFILE

Name: Mikey Chan

Hometown: Aurora, Illinois

Physical description: 5'7", 205 lbs., black hair, brown eyes.

Occupation: Student

Background: Older of two brothers. Parents both work in medical field. B student, no record of trouble.

It seemed like five minutes after I fell asleep that I heard a loud, annoying buzzing. It was coming through the mansion's intercom system. Did I mention it was loud?

"Dude, you gotta be kidding me." James sat up in his bed and stretched. "Is that this show's idea of an alarm clock?"

Our other roommate, Mikey, was nothing more than a lump under the covers. "What time is it?" he mumbled.

"Don't ask." I glanced at the window. It was still dark outside.

"Up and at 'em, fat boy!" James sounded more awake already. He must have remembered there was a competition that morning. The guy is all about competition. "I call first shower."

It was finally getting light as we gathered out in the yard a short while later. Everyone still looked a little rumpled and sleepy. Everyone except Ripley. I caught her yawning once or twice, but otherwise she looked just as pulled-together as always. They must teach that in celebrity-heiress school.

Oops, scratch that. There was one other person who looked like her usual self. Veronica. She was dressed in a form-fitting yellow suit, and her lipstick was so red it practically glowed.

She strode out and stood in front of us. "Good morning, everyone," she said. "I hope you're all feeling well rested. Now follow me, please. This morning's competition is called Junk in the Trunk."

A few people laughed at the name. The rest just wandered after Veronica, yawning or looking tired and hungry. We hadn't been allowed to eat breakfast yet. When I'd stopped in the kitchen, planning to grab a granola bar or something, one of the cameramen had been there to stop me. We weren't allowed to eat until after the competition.

Veronica led us around some bushes behind the woodpile. That's when we saw the setup for the competition. Rubber flooring about the size of a room was laid out on the grass, and a bunch of huge trash cans were clustered in the middle of it.

Weirder still, a dozen wooden trunks formed a circle about seven feet overhead. They were dangling from wires and swaying back and forth in the breeze. Each trunk had one of our names painted on the bottom.

"Junk in the Trunk." Hal pointed to the swinging trunks overhead. I guess he'd returned to planet Earth long enough to pay attention. "I get it!"

"Congrats, genius. Now shut up so we can hear how I'm going to kick your butts this time." James grinned confidently at Veronica. "So what do we have to do? Lay it on us."

She raised an eyebrow at him. "Thank you, Mr. Sittenfeld," she said icily. "If you hadn't said that, I'd have no idea what to say next." Then she surveyed the rest of us. "This competition involves one of your deprivations—junk food." She pointed one very red fingernail at the trash cans on the ground. "Those are filled to the brim with potato chips."

Mikey let out a little squeak. His eyes were very round as he stared at the cans.

"You will see that you each have a trunk." This time Veronica pointed up. "When the buzzer sounds, those trunks will start moving around in a circle. Your task is to toss potato chips up into your individual trunks. Make sure your aim is good— if you miss and hit someone else's trunk, good for them, bad for you. The contestant whose trunk weighs the most when the buzzer sounds again is the winner and gets to choose the next deprivation for the house. Everyone else will have to clean up the rest of the chips from the yard."

"Sounds great." Mikey licked his lips. "Let's get started!"

"Oh, one more thing." Veronica lifted one finger. "During this challenge—*and* the cleanup afterward—you aren't allowed to eat a single bite. You can't even lick the grease and salt off your fingers. Anyone who is caught doing so has to go without meals today and tomorrow—stale bread and water only. Plus he, she, or they must do all food-related chores, including cooking for the rest of the house, for the same period of time."

"Too bad for you, chubs," James taunted Mikey. "Listen, when you're on food duty tomorrow, make sure you remember I like extra tomato on my sandwiches."

I glanced at Mikey. His face had fallen and he looked sort of sick.

I couldn't really blame him. My stomach was grumbling a bit too. No wonder they hadn't wanted us to eat breakfast.

"Don't bother trying to cheat, either, kids." It was Sylvia, the hyper PA. "I'll be keeping an eye on you." She was holding a cup of coffee and a dough-nut. She smirked and took a big bite.

"Yes, and so will the rest of us, not to mention the cameras," Veronica added. "Even if you think you've gotten away with it, don't be so sure. We'll be reviewing the footage carefully."

BZZZT! The buzzer sounded, and the contest was on.

I raced toward the trash cans with the others. James flung the lid off one and grabbed a huge handful of potato chips. The scent of grease wafted out. Mikey let out a moan.

"You can do it, Mikey," Brynn murmured to him as she dug both hands into another can. "Stay strong."

I smiled at her. I already knew she was cool, but it was amazing how she just kept getting cooler.

Then I got down to business. Have you ever tried to toss potato chips seven feet into the air and hit a moving target? Let me tell you, it's not easy. Especially when it's breezy. It didn't help that we all kept bumping into one another as we chased our trunks, staring upward.

"Flip them with your thumb like you're tossing a coin," Frank murmured as he rushed past me on his way back to get more chips.

That trick worked—sort of. I still only hit my

trunk about once out of every fifteen tries. If that. My only comfort was that, judging by the cursing and cries of annoyance from all around, nobody else was doing much better.

I was sort of relieved when the buzzer went off again, ending the contest. "Everybody stop!" Veronica commanded.

"Hey!" shouted Gail, pointing. "Did you guys see that? Cheater! Ripley just ate a chip!"

A Guy Who Can Handle Stuff

I think everyone was pretty surprised that Ripley was the one to cave. We all thought it would be Mikey. Ripley shot Gail an evil look for ratting her out, but then she fessed up.

"Sorry," she said, tossing her long, straight brown hair over her shoulder. "I just couldn't resist."

She didn't really look that sorry. But maybe that was just her. She's used to getting in trouble, and she's used to having her parents' money and connections get her out of it.

That wasn't going to be the case this time. Veronica immediately sent her inside to prepare breakfast for the rest of us.

"But nothing but water for you," she warned her.

"The cameras will be watching. Someone will bring you some bread later on." Veronica patted her sleek blond hair. "Don't be surprised if it's a little stale."

"Fine, whatever." Ripley headed inside.

Meanwhile the rest of us were wondering who had won. It only took a few minutes for the verdict to come back.

"It was close," announced Veronica. "But our winner is . . . Frank Dooley."

"Aw, man!" James exclaimed with a scowl.

The others all managed a cheer or a "congrats," even though most of them didn't look too happy. I wasn't feeling too happy myself. After helping nab Mitch, I wasn't sure it was a good idea to draw more attention to myself. Guess I should've thought about that before the competition.

"Frank, I'll expect to hear your decision on the next deprivation tomorrow morning at breakfast," Veronica said. "As for the rest of you, you might want to enjoy your favorite luxuries today. It might be your last chance." With one last evil smile, she strode away.

"Nicely played, bro." Joe came up and clapped me on the back. "What are you going to choose?"

"I don't know yet." As we stepped into the house, Brynn caught up with us.

"Hey," she said. "So how about Ripley eating that

chip? Talk about a surprise! As thin as she is, I'm surprised she even knows what a chip is."

"Maybe that was the problem," Joe joked. "She wasn't sure what Veronica was talking about, and she ate it by accident."

I chuckled. Before I could say anything, Bobby T caught up to us.

"Frank, old buddy, old pal," he said, giving me a friendly punch on the arm.

"Hi, Bobby," I said. "What's up?"

As if I didn't know. I was pretty sure just about everyone in the house would be my best friend for the next twenty-four hours.

"Not much," he said. "Just wondering if, you know, you've got any thoughts about that next deprivation. Such as, say, *not* getting rid of our Internet service."

Joe grinned. "Subtle, dude," he told Bobby. Then he glanced at Brynn. "Want to go see if there are any granola bars left in the supply closet?" he said. "I don't know about you, but I'm not looking forward to seeing what Ripley comes up with for breakfast. She grew up with servants—I'd be surprised if she even knows how to pour a glass of OJ."

"Sure. I could use a snack." Brynn glanced at me and smiled. "Want to come, Frank?"

Joe looked surprised. I was a little surprised

myself. Since when did Brynn invite me along with her and Joe? Sure, we'd had that nice moment after she got freaked out in the kitchen. But those two had been tight pretty much since day one.

"Um, sure," I said. "Let's all go look for those granola bars."

For the rest of the day, Brynn stuck to me like glue. At first it was kind of awkward. As Joe likes to tell anyone who'll listen, I'm not that great with girls.

But like I said, Brynn was different. She was so easy to talk to that before long I practically forgot she was a girl. Well, okay, not really. You'd have to be blind and deaf to forget that. After a while I was almost sorry that her new interest in me would probably end as soon as I announced my decision on the next deprivation.

"So what do you think I should pick tomorrow?" I asked her as the two of us stacked wood on the hearth of the gigantic fireplace in the great room. James and Joe were out getting more. I was in no hurry to rejoin them. Lugging firewood up the stairs isn't much fun.

She just shrugged. "Oh, I don't know," she said. "It's up to you. I haven't really thought about it."

"Really? You mean you don't have an opinion for me like everyone else does?" I went for that jokey, breezy tone Joe likes to use with girls. It didn't really work for me, though. I just sounded like a dork.

"Is that why you think I'm hanging around?" She tilted her head at me. Her eyes locked on mine, which made me sort of forget how to breathe for a second. "That's not it at all. It's just that you really seem like a guy who can handle stuff, you know? I mean, you were the one who pulled that dead guy out of the pool at the first challenge. And you rescued your brother and those other guys when they got trapped in the sauna last week and almost died. You even helped catch that guy Mitch." She reached over and put a hand on my arm. Her touch felt cool and soft. "With everything that's happened, being in this house makes me nervous. But being with you makes me feel safer."

Out of the corner of my eye, I saw Joe heading toward us with an armful of firewood. I wondered how much he'd heard. Judging by the look on his face, probably too much.

"What's up, you two?" Joe's pretty good at that jokey, breezy thing. Anybody but me probably wouldn't have noticed the edge in his voice.

Brynn finished her stacking. "There," she said, brushing off her palms. "I'll be right back, okay? I'm going to wash my hands."

As soon as she was gone, Joe dumped the wood

he was holding and rounded on me. "Hey, what's the deal?" he demanded. "So a girl likes me better for once. Do you have to try to steal her away just to prove you can?"

"Don't be an idiot. Brynn and I are just friends."

He rolled his eyes. "Yeah. If that," he snapped. "Get a clue, bro. She's just trying to influence your decision about the next deprivation."

I couldn't help a flash of annoyance. "In case you haven't noticed while you were drooling all over her, she's not like that, Joe," I retorted. "She's just feeling a little nervous and wants to be around someone who makes her feel safe. Not my fault if that's me."

"Uh-huh, sure." Joe rolled his eyes. "Believe that if you want. Just don't be surprised when she suddenly starts feeling a lot safer, oh, around breakfast time tomorrow."

He stomped away. I sighed and went back to stacking wood.

"Seriously, though," I said to Brynn. "What should I do tomorrow? I don't have much longer to decide, and I still have no clue."

It was around three in the afternoon. We were hanging out in the kitchen. Brynn was flipping through a magazine and I was eating an apple. Not surprisingly, Ripley hadn't turned out to be much of a cook. We'd had tuna sandwiches for lunch. That normally wouldn't be a bad thing, since I like a good tuna sandwich. However, these were *not* good tuna sandwiches.

"I don't know." Brynn shrugged and glanced over at the deprivation list posted on the wall. "Um, I guess you could always pick something like magazines"—she waved the one she was holding—"or, like, radio. Or how about TV? We only get two hours a day as it is. That would probably be missed a lot less than most of the other stuff on the list."

"That makes sense, I guess." I chuckled. "Somehow, though, I don't think Mikey would see the logic."

That reminded me. I hadn't seen Mikey since lunchtime. Ever since the ice incident, Joe and I were keeping an eye on him. I still wasn't sure he made the best suspect, but you never know.

All morning it had been easy to keep track of him. He'd taken every opportunity to make suggestions about what I should do. Basically, he was campaigning hard to keep not only his beloved TV, but also all our remaining food-related luxuries. Even though we'd already lost junk food and hot food, there were a few more items on the list. Salt and spices. Utensils—knives, forks, and spoons. Milk and OJ and pretty much all beverages besides soda.

Brynn flipped another page in her magazine. "I guess," she said. "He'd probably be the only one who'd care about losing TV, though."

I wasn't so sure about that. Still, it was kind of tempting to do it anyway. If Mikey was our culprit, upsetting him like that might be a good way to draw him out.

Just then I saw Joe walk by in the hallway. "I'll be back in a sec," I told Brynn. "Uh, bathroom. You know."

I hurried out of the room and caught up to Joe. "Yo," he greeted me, sounding a little sour.

He'd probably seen me sitting in there with Brynn. But I didn't have time to worry about it.

"Listen," I said. "Have you seen Mikey lately?"

Joe shook his head. "He disappeared right after lunch. Why? Think he's up to something?"

"Maybe. Then again, he could just be avoiding James."

"Yeah," Joe agreed. "Totally understandable. I'd like to avoid James more myself. He's been in the great room for the past half hour bragging about how much he can bench-press."

"No wonder Mikey's been under our radar until now," I mused. "Half the time he's not around."

Joe headed back toward the great room. I headed

for the bedrooms. Mikey wasn't in any of them, or in the bathroom, either.

I was coming back down the dramatic S-shaped staircase when I heard a door open. Looking over into what used to be the billiards room, I spotted Mikey. He was coming out of the Deprivation Chamber—the podlike structure where we were supposed to go if we wanted to vent to the cameras about anything. Joe and I had made a point of going in there a time or two each. We figured it would make our fake IDs stronger if we pretended to complain about each other and how hard it was to be reunited in front of the cameras and stuff.

Anyway, at the moment Mikey looked angry. He saw me standing there and hurried over.

"Ripley's a cheat!" he burst out.

"Huh?" I knew he liked potato chips. Was he really holding that much of a grudge about Ripley for eating one that morning?

He was practically quivering with outrage. "I was just heading in there to, uh . . ." He shot me a sidelong glance. "Well, I heard you might be thinking of depriving us of TV, so, you know . . ."

He looked momentarily sheepish. It didn't take an undercover agent to figure out he'd been planning to complain about me.

"Anyway," he went on, his fury returning quickly,

"Ripley was coming out just as I was going in. And when I got inside, I swear I smelled food—*real* food. *Cooked* food. Not just gross tuna sandwiches." He scowled, glancing over his shoulder at the chamber. "I think she was eating in there!"

Suspicious Behavior

When Frank told me about Mikey's accusation, I couldn't really get too worked up about it. "So Ripley was sneaking some pasta or whatever," I said. "So what? Her parents probably bribed the producers or something. That Sylvia chick would probably do it for fifty bucks."

Frank shrugged. "Maybe. Still, it's one more thing to add to the list of suspicious behavior."

"Good point. Besides, the rest of our suspect list is pretty weak."

Something else was weak too. Frank. Specifically, the way he couldn't see that Brynn didn't really care about him. But I tried not to think about that. Frank and I were here to do a job—I couldn't let his total cluelessness about girls get in the way.

Just then someone pounded on the door of the bathroom. "Hey!" It was James, of course. All those cuts in his mouth hadn't made him any quieter. "Hurry up in there!"

That was the end of our private discussion. We left the bathroom and parted ways.

SUSPECT PROFILE

Name: Ripley Lansing

Hometown: Malibu, California

Physical description: 5'10", 140 lbs., brown hair, blue eyes.

Occupation: High school student/celebrity heiress

Background: Rock star dad, CEO mom. Two brothers. Ripley is the family's black sheep and wild child.

Suspicious behavior: Might be in cahoots with Veronica and/or the producers.

Suspected of: Causing mayhem in the house for ratings.

Possible motive: Could be going along with the producers' plans in exchange for a sympathetic edit on the show—which would help her convince her parents not to cut off her funds.

I was still thinking about Ripley. We'd been suspicious of her all along. But we hadn't done much about it. Maybe it was time to change that.

I found her in the kitchen. She was chopping up some lettuce and stuff.

"Hey," I greeted her. "What are you doing?"

"What does it look like?" She flipped her long hair over her shoulder and shot me a glance. "It takes a long time to fix food for twelve people, you know."

"Yeah." I slid onto one of the barstools at the counter. "Sorry I can't offer to help you. But I can hang out and give you some moral support if you want."

"Are you really that bored?"

I grinned. "Actually, I'm sort of avoiding someone."

"Really?" She tossed a handful of lettuce into a big salad bowl. "Let me guess—your long-lost brother, right? Is he trying to make you feel guilty for having nice things? I get that all the time."

"Yeah, he's a pain in the neck. But that's not it this time." I shrugged. "Actually, it's Mikey. He's been complaining all afternoon 'cause he smelled food in the Deprivation Chamber." I chuckled. "Guess it drove him nuts."

"Hmm." Ripley wiped off her knife, then started slicing a tomato.

"Hey, come to think of it, he said you were in there too. Did you smell anything, or is Mikey just hallucinating from hunger?" I was careful to keep my voice casual.

Ripley shot me a sharp look. "Let me guess," she snapped. "Mikey's going around telling everyone I was sneaking food in there, right? And the others sent you in to try to find out if it's true?"

Oops. Not casual enough, I guess. "Um, no, that's not it, I . . . ," I stammered.

"Well, Mikey is the sneaky one if you ask me!" She frowned. "Just this morning I caught him huddled in the girls' shower when nobody was around. He acted really weird about it too." She rolled her eyes. "Either he's the world's stupidest Peeping Tom, or he's up to something else."

"Really?" My mind flashed back to the times Frank and I had come across Mikey in odd places. It was looking more and more like a pattern.

The *click-click* of high heels on tile broke into my thoughts. Veronica swooped into the room.

"Sorry to interrupt," she said briskly, as usual not sounding sorry at all. "Ms. Lansing, I need you to come with me to the Deprivation Chamber, please. We'd like you to make some remarks about your punishment."

"Whatever." Ripley wiped off her hands on

a towel. Then she followed Veronica out of the kitchen.

I trailed along behind them. I wasn't sure whether to believe what Ripley had just said about Mikey. But if it was true, I wanted to find out more.

They were just disappearing into the chamber when I got there. I hung around just outside, figuring it would only take a few minutes to record their little Q & A.

But I was wrong. Ten minutes passed, then fifteen. How much could Ripley have to say about cooking, anyway?

Weird, I thought, remembering Mikey's accusation. Maybe I would just have to go in there when Ripley came out and see what I could smell. I still wasn't sure what sneaking food could possibly have to do with the other stuff going on in the house. But if that's what she was doing in there, it now seemed that Veronica was involved. It was more than a little weird that the host was still in there with Ripley. Normally Veronica wasn't supposed to hear what anyone said inside the Deprivation Chamber— those comments weren't supposed to influence her decision about who to kick out. So what were they doing in there?

I had plenty of time to think about it. It was a good half hour before the door opened again and

Veronica and Ripley came out. By then I'd come up with a theory or two.

Veronica spotted me right away. "Mr. Carr," she said. "You appear not to have enough to do."

"Oh, um, no," I said. "I just wanted to go in there." I took a step toward the chamber. "Uh, see, my so-called brother keeps griping about how my sneakers were more expensive than his whole house, and I really need to vent about it."

I figured that would do the trick. The producers love any whiff of interpersonal drama. Isn't that what reality TV is all about?

But Veronica didn't seem impressed. "That can wait." She stepped into my path, neatly blocking me from getting any closer to the chamber. "Right now, I'll have to ask you to come with me. There are some boxes you can help me bring up from the storeroom."

By the time everyone started talking about getting ready for bed, I could tell that Frank was stressing. We met up in the supply closet for a quick rendezvous.

I filled him in on my chat with Ripley and what had happened afterward. "What if she's in cahoots with the producers?" I finished. "Like Olivia said, maybe they're afraid the show won't be dramatic enough if they don't spice things up."

"Seems kind of nuts, but I guess you never know." Frank seemed a little distracted. "But listen, I still haven't figured out what to do tomorrow. Any deprivation I pick is going to make someone freak out."

"Yeah. Except maybe the new girl, Gail Digby," I joked. "The way she talks, even the air we breathe is a luxury."

Frank blinked. "Hey, that reminds me," he said. "Brynn told me something kind of interesting about Gail."

I couldn't help it. I winced a little when he said Brynn's name. "Oh yeah?" I tried not to show I was bothered. "What?"

"Olivia told her that Gail's dad went to jail for arson a few years back."

"Yeah, well, Olivia would say just about anything to win," I pointed out. "She's probably getting desperate, since her little alliance isn't working out so well." Earlier in the game, Olivia had approached Frank about forming an alliance. She'd also wanted to include this guy Wilson, who dropped out shortly afterward.

Frank nodded. "Still, if it's true, it adds a wrinkle," he said. "Think about it. Nobody needs that prize money more than Gail. It would be life-changing for her."

"It would be life-changing for me, too. I could finally trade in my motorcycle for that Porsche we saw at the car show last month."

"Focus, Joe." Frank sounded every inch the stuffy big brother. "You know we're not here for that. Anyway, this new round of mischief started around the same time Gail came into the game."

He had a point. "Yeah," I said thoughtfully. "And this time it *is* just mischief. Well, aside from that glass ice incident . . ." Would Gail really do something like that? Who could say? We really didn't know these people at all. "Plus, don't forget Gail was the one who tattled on Ripley during the challenge this morning," I added. "She could be trying to take out the competition any way she can. But could she have sent everyone those threatening letters way back when?"

"Maybe. Depends on whether she knew from the beginning that she was joining the show." Frank shrugged. "Either way, let's keep an eye on her."

"Got it." I nodded. "So it's looking like Ripley, Mikey, and Gail are our top suspects. Plus maybe Veronica and the producers, though I really can't see them pulling that ice trick."

"Yeah." Frank checked his watch. "We don't want to stay in here too long. If Ripley has been noticing Mikey skulking around, she might start to wonder about us, too. Maybe we can talk about this more tomorrow."

We left the closet and headed upstairs. When we passed the girls' bathroom, the door was open, and I looked in. Call it a reflex.

"Oh my God!" I choked out. "Brynn!"

Brynn looked up at me from over near the sink. Her eyes were wide and her face pale. The rest of her was covered in blood.

Double Trouble

I followed Joe as he raced into the bathroom. "What happened?" I asked Brynn.

She held up both hands and stared at them. They were slick and red with blood.

"I—I was just going to brush my hair," she said, seeming stunned.

Luckily, Joe and I are trained to handle people in just these sorts of situations. He took her by the shoulder and gently pushed her down onto the vanity bench. Meanwhile I was already grabbing a washcloth off the towel rack. Whoever it belonged to probably wouldn't be happy, but oh well.

"Where's the blood coming from?" I asked. She was still staring at her hands, and I guessed that was my answer. There was no blood at all on her face or neck; it was mostly on her hands and running down her arms. Some had also dripped onto her shirt and jeans.

"I—I stuck my hands into my makeup bag without looking—I just wanted to grab my brush." She gestured toward a large pink fabric case on the counter. The movement made more blood pulse out of her hand. I grabbed it and started trying to stop the flow. "Something inside cut me."

Joe hurried over and looked into the bag. "Knives," he said grimly. "There are, like, five steak knives stuck in here, sharp end up."

"That would do it." I dabbed at Brynn's hands with the washcloth, which was already soaked. "Call the medics, Joe."

"No!" Brynn looked alarmed. "I'll be okay. The bleeding's already stopping. I'll just wash off and put some bandages on the cuts."

Joe was still peering into the makeup bag. "Who would do something like this?" he murmured. I shot him a look, not wanting him to do too much thinking aloud in front of Brynn.

But at the moment I was more concerned for Brynn than I was about the case. "You could be going into shock," I told her. "You really should let the medics take a look."

"No, seriously. I'm okay now. I was just surprised, that's all." To prove her point, she stood up and went over to the sink. She started washing off the blood. "The cuts aren't even that deep. And I'm tougher than I look." She forced a smile.

"I'll, uh, go get some more bandages from the supply closet," Joe offered. On his way out, he shot me a meaningful look. I guessed he was going to check out where everybody was and who might have planted the knives.

I probably should have done the same. But I was still too worried about Brynn to leave her alone. Despite the brave face she was putting on, I could see that her hands were shaking.

"Are you sure you don't want the medics?" I asked.

"Positive." She gave me a wan smile. "I already feel better with you here."

I had no idea what to say to that. So I just helped her clean up her hands. She was right—the cuts weren't very bad, despite all the blood. A glance into her bag showed that she'd been lucky not to do more damage.

"There." Brynn finished wrapping the last bandage around her pinky finger. "I'll be good as new in a few days."

"I hope so. Want me to deprive the house of

utensils tomorrow morning so this won't happen again?" I asked, only half joking.

She shot me a sympathetic look. "You haven't decided which deprivation to choose yet, huh?"

"It's no big deal." I didn't want to obsess over something so stupid when she'd just been hurt. But when one of her archy eyebrows popped up skeptically, I laughed. "Okay, yeah," I admitted. "I still have no idea what to do, and it's stressing me out."

She patted the vanity bench beside her. "Here, sit down and tell me about it," she said. "You've been so sweet to me—the least I can do is try to help you in return."

What else could I do? I sat down. The vanity bench was built to hold two people. Even so, we were close. Really, really close. I only hoped she couldn't see me start to sweat.

"So last I heard, you were thinking about my idea to get rid of TV," Brynn started. "What are your other options?"

She rested her hand on the bench between us. It was only, like, an inch from my pant leg. My eyes kept wandering down to it.

"Um . . . ," I began.

So much for feeling normal around Brynn. Sitting this close to her, I have to admit, it was hard not to notice that she was really something special.

Usually Joe doesn't have the most discriminating taste in girls. Basically, any girl who will give him the time of day is A-OK with him.

But he'd struck gold this time. And I wasn't sure he even realized it. In fact, I seriously doubted it.

Still, I couldn't help feeling guilty. Not because Brynn was smiling at me as if I was the coolest guy on the planet—I couldn't help that. It was more about how *I* was thinking about *her*. Because all of a sudden, what I was thinking was how easy it would be to just lean over and kiss her right here and now. . . .

Maybe I actually would have fought off my nerves and done it. Maybe not. I never got the chance to find out.

That's because a sudden loud, terrified scream rang out from somewhere outside. Brynn jumped.

"Who was that?" she asked.

I was already on my feet. "Let's go find out."

People were running from all corners of the house. We all got down to the rear foyer—in a mansion like that, it seemed weird to call it a mudroom—at about the same time. Mary Moore was standing in the open doorway.

"What happened?" Olivia demanded. "Mary, was that you screaming? You just about gave me a heart attack!"

"S-sorry," Mary gasped out. She looked tinier and paler than ever. It was dark out, and she took another step into the light. That was when I saw that she was covered in mud and her long, straight hair was tangled and dirty.

The others saw it too. "What happened to you?" Bobby T exclaimed.

"I was out in the yard taking out the trash." A sob escaped as Mary spoke. "While I was at the garbage cans, I saw a little girl standing at the far end of the yard near the woodpile."

"A little girl?" Hal wrinkled his nose in confusion. "Who was it?"

"Hush," Ripley chided him. "She's trying to tell us!"

Mary swallowed hard. "I called out to her, but she didn't answer. It was hard to see in the dark, but she sort of, you know, beckoned to me. I thought she might be lost or something, so I took a few steps that way." She sobbed again, her eyes filling with tears. "That's when someone grabbed me from behind and shoved me to the ground!"

The Fangs Come Out

The house was in an uproar after Mary's story. I immediately turned and raced out into the yard. Frank was right beside me. James, Ripley, and Gail were only a few steps behind.

"Look for anything suspicious," I told them, already heading for the far end of the yard.

It was pretty dark out there without even a flashlight to help us. We didn't find any signs of a little girl—or anyone else. Just Mary's dropped bag of trash near the garbage cans.

When we headed back in, everyone else was still talking about Mary's scary encounter. "I bet there was no little girl at all," James said with a snort. "She prob'ly just saw a snake or some other creepy crawly by the garbage cans and made up that tall tale to cover for her own wimpiness." He smirked and winked at Bobby T. "You know how girls are."

Mary frowned. "Tell me, James." Her voice was as soft as ever, though it held an edge of steel. "Have *you* ever helped milk the venom out of a Western diamondback rattlesnake's fangs? Because *I* have."

James blinked at her in surprise. For once he didn't seem to have a comeback.

I exchanged an amused glance with Frank behind James's back. Go, homeschool-girl!

Meanwhile, Hal looked impressed. "Have you really done that?" he asked.

Mary shrugged, suddenly back to her usual meek self. "It was no big deal," she said quietly. "Just part of a unit on herpetology."

Just then Olivia noticed the bandages on Brynn's hands. "Hey, what happened to you?"

"I cut myself." Brynn sounded distracted. She was staring at Mary, looking anxious.

"Whoa!" Bobby T took in the number of bandages on Brynn's fingers and hands. "What did you cut yourself *on*, a chain saw?" He shook his head and started pacing. "You know, I'm starting to have a really bad feeling about this place. Too much freaky crap is going on around here."

"I know what you mean." Brynn bit her lip. "It's

like this place is—I don't know, cursed or something."

"Yeah, go ahead and believe that if you want," James scoffed. "You can believe it all the way home, while I stay here and grab the mil." He seemed to have recovered from Mary's smackdown already.

Bobby barely seemed to hear him. "This is getting ridiculous," he said, still pacing. "I mean, it was one thing when it was dead birds and goofy messages, right? But first Sittenfeld gets his mouth all cut up, and now Mary gets attacked, and Brynn . . ." He waved a hand toward Brynn's bandages, not even seeming to care anymore about the details of what had happened to her. "I'm thinking it's just not worth it anymore."

Mary nodded and bit her lip. "The next person to drop out gets thirty thousand dollars, right?" she asked, looking around at the rest of us.

Mikey gasped. "You're not thinking of taking it, are you?"

"Maybe." Mary shrugged and glanced over her shoulder at the darkness outside.

I hated the thought that whoever was doing this might actually succeed in scaring people away. "No way," I told Mary. "You've got to stay. Otherwise whoever's doing this wins, and you don't want that, right?"

"I don't know. . . ." Mary still looked nervous.

But I wasn't about to give up. With a little help from Frank, Mikey, and Hal, I eventually talked her down. She agreed to stay—at least for now.

She seemed to relax and go back to normal after that. But I soon realized that, while she might not be showing it as much, Brynn was still pretty freaked out. She made both me and Frank walk her back upstairs.

"I just don't feel safe by myself anymore," she said, her voice shaking. "I don't want to go anywhere alone. Not even the bathroom or the Deprivation Chamber." She wrapped her arms around herself and shivered. "I'm half tempted to do what Mary was saying—take the money and get out of here tonight."

"Aw, come on." I was horrified by the thought that she might leave. But I did my best to hide it. "Aren't you even curious to see what horrible new deprivation Frank lays on us tomorrow morning?" I joked weakly.

"Yeah." Frank smiled hopefully at her. "Tell you what, Brynn. If you promise to stick around, I'll do like you suggested and cut the rest of our TV." He grinned. "I'll just have to deal with Mikey somehow."

I shot him a surprised look. Was he nuts? If he

cut our remaining TV privileges, it wasn't only Mikey who was going to be upset. That made-for-TV movie about the murder in the mansion was on tomorrow night. At least half the people in the house were looking forward to watching it.

But when Brynn's face brightened, I held my tongue. "Really?" she asked Frank with a small smile. "You really think it was a good idea?"

"Sure," he said, giving her a goofy grin.

I had to hold back a grimace myself. Somehow, I doubted he'd be feeling so great about it when the others heard his plan.

Sure enough, when Frank announced his decision, it was greeted by groans and scowls and muttered curses. The only ones who didn't seem upset were Brynn, Gail, and Ripley. Oh, and Bobby T, of course, who just seemed relieved that his precious Internet connection was safe.

"More cereal, anyone?" Ripley asked cheerfully.

She'd been bizarrely chipper all morning. Maybe all that cooking was actually giving her a purpose in life. She even *looked* different. Her dark hair was usually as sleek and smooth as a mink coat. But today she was sporting a bunch of wild waves. She'd explained that it was a new hairdo in honor of her role as house chef.

"I can't believe you're doing this to me," Mikey moaned, pushing away his plate of cold-water oatmeal.

"Not just you." Olivia shook her head and scowled at Frank. "That *Witness to Evil* movie's on tonight, remember? We were all going to watch."

"I wasn't," Gail put in. She hadn't stopped eating all through Frank's announcement.

"Sorry to interrupt your television schedule, everyone," Veronica put in with her trademark smirk. "But the TV set is being removed from the great room as we speak. Enjoy your breakfast."

Most of the house seemed to get over their disappointment by the time breakfast was over. But not Mikey. He eventually started eating again, but he stayed pretty cranky. I saw him shoot Frank an evil look or ten, though I'm not sure Frank noticed.

After the meal, when everyone scattered, Frank and I slipped away and headed outside. We wanted to check out the yard again to see if we could find any evidence of Mary's attacker. It had been pretty dark out there last night. We easily could have missed something.

But even in broad daylight, we didn't find anything. The culprit had covered his or her tracks well.

"It's strange." Frank crouched down, staring at the ground near the woodpile. "It rained the other night, and the ground is still soft. If anyone was standing around here, they should've left prints."

"Even a little girl?" I wasn't sure I believed there had been a real little girl out there. But someone could have draped a shirt on a stick or something, maybe. "Anyone light enough might not leave prints, even on soft ground."

"True." Frank looked thoughtful. "Mary's quite light herself, and the only sign she was out here is the spot where she fell. So who else is a lightweight?"

"Silent Girl. Ripley, maybe—she's tall, but she's almost as skinny as Mary. Even Hal—he's practically a stick figure." I shrugged. "Then again, it could just be someone who knew enough to erase their tracks."

"Yeah." Frank's shoulders slumped. "Which equals anyone sneaky enough to pull off all these stunts in the first place."

We gave up and went back inside. Brynn was just coming down the stairs. "Hey," she greeted us. "Anyone feel like going for a walk? I could use some fresh air."

"Sure," Frank spoke up right away.

He's such a total Eagle Scout that he's always the

first one to offer to help anyone with anything. But on this particular occasion he sounded a little *too* eager to help out.

"No," I blurted out. "Er, I mean, that's okay. I was just about to head outside for some fresh air myself." That didn't make much sense, considering I'd just come *in*side. But I've never let a little thing like logic stop me when there's a cute girl on the line. "I'll go."

I gave Frank a look, silently daring him to argue. He just frowned.

"Whatever," he muttered. "Have fun, you two."

Logged Out

"**W**hat are you doing?"
I looked up at Joe. "What does it look like?" I waved the book I was reading.

"Whatever, dude. Just asking," he muttered.

I sighed. Things had been a little tense between us for the past day or so. It had started with that walk Joe had taken with Brynn. I admit it—I was starting to think about her. A lot. I was trying not to let it interfere with the case, but it was kind of hard. Especially when Joe kept wandering off with her every chance he got.

It didn't help that absolutely nothing interesting had happened in the house since breakfast the day before. We'd barely even seen Veronica since my deprivation announcement. At least the mansion had a well-stocked library. I'd spent a lot of time sitting in front of the fire with a book. For one thing, that made it easy to observe my housemates as they wandered in and out of the great room. Although it *was* a little uncomfortable when Mikey would come in, stare sadly at the spot where the TV had been, then turn to glare at me.

I didn't care if Mikey was annoyed with me. But being at odds with my brother was getting old. I closed my book and stood up.

"Hey," I told Joe. "Let's, um, go see if there's any bottled water left in the supply closet."

"Okay."

I was in the lead as we rounded the corner. Mikey was just stepping out of the closet. He sort of jumped when he spotted us.

"Oh! Hey, guys," he said. "I was just in there getting more, uh, toilet paper."

"Really?" said Joe. "Where is it?"

Mikey glanced down at his empty hands. "Oh. Um, when I got in there I remembered I already got some."

He hurried off. Joe and I let ourselves into the closet.

"That was weird," he said. "Mikey, I mean."

"Yeah." I did want to talk about the case. But

first I had something else to say. "Listen, Joe. About Brynn . . ."

"What about her?" he demanded, instantly suspicious.

I held up both hands. "Chill, man. I'm just saying we can't let her distract us, okay? We're supposed to be working here."

He shrugged. "If you say so."

He still sounded pretty tense. Fine. I wasn't going to jolly him out of it this time. He was a big boy—he would just have to deal.

"Okay, we should probably talk about the latest incident—Mary getting shoved out by the woodpile."

"What about it?" Joe shook his head. "We already decided that was a dead end for now. Anyway, I think we should talk about Mikey. He's been acting weirder and weirder. I think he should be on the top of the suspect list."

"Maybe," I said.

"Too bad you had to go and tick him off by taking away his precious TV," Joe added. "It would be a lot easier to question him if he wasn't moping around."

"Look, Joe," I said with a flash of irritation. "If you're mad about something, why don't you just come out and—"

The door swung open. "There you guys are!" Ripley was standing there, smiling at us from beneath the brim of her latest hat.

Oh, right. I forgot to mention that *one* thing had happened in the house in the past twenty-four hours. Ripley had started wearing hats.

Okay, I'll admit it. I should have noticed sooner, being a trained detective and all. I guess fashion stuff just doesn't stand out to me. But the other girls had complimented her at breakfast on her little beret-type cap thingy. Then later, when she turned up in some kind of sparkly cowboy hat, James had made some obnoxious comments.

Ripley had ignored him. She just kept saying she was "going to make hats cool again." Whatever that meant. Maybe she thought they looked better with her new curly hairdo or something. Who knows how girls like Ripley think?

"Were you looking for us?" Joe asked her. "Is there a surprise competition or something?"

"Not right now." She glanced up and down the hall, then leaned closer. "But I heard there's going to be one tomorrow. And then an elimination right afterward."

"Really?" I was surprised. "But it hasn't been a full week yet since the last elimination."

Joe shot me a look. "Lighten up, Frank," he said.

"Not everybody schedules their whole lives down to the second like you do."

I gritted my teeth, resisting the urge to snap back at him. It was weird—Joe and I don't argue very often. But when we do, he can get under my skin like nobody else.

"So is that what you were coming to tell us?" I asked Ripley.

"Oh! No," she said. "Mary just told me Veronica ordered someone to bring in more wood for the fire right now." She shrugged. "Mary's afraid to go out there by the woodpile after what happened, and I figured I worked hard enough yesterday doing all the cooking." She reached out and touched me lightly on the arm. "So tag! You're it."

"Okay, I'm on it." Joe and I weren't accomplishing much anyway. Maybe a little manual labor would clear my head. Besides, I still couldn't believe there wasn't some little clue we'd missed out there where Mary had been attacked. That was another thing I'd learned working with ATAC. The bad guys almost always mess up something, even if it's just the tiniest detail. If you can find their mistake, you can nab them.

Joe didn't offer to come out and help. Maybe he was feeling as sick of me as I was of him right then. Or maybe he was planning to run off and find

Brynn. I tried not to think about it as I headed outside.

It had been a chilly day, with showers off and on. Nobody else was outside.

I wandered across the yard, trying to gauge the distance from the garbage cans to the woodpile. Maybe thirty yards, give or take. Had it really been a little girl Mary had seen? If not, what *had* she seen? Had someone from the mansion pushed her down? It had been pretty chaotic right afterward—it wasn't too hard to believe that someone could've slipped in and joined the crowd.

I had reached the woodpile by now. As I grabbed a log, I heard an odd sound. What was that?

Pausing, I cocked my head. Was I going crazy? Or had that sounded like . . . a little girl laughing?

I held my breath, hoping to hear it again. Instead, I heard an ominous rumble.

"No!" I shouted, starting to jump backward.

But it was too late. The entire woodpile came crashing down on top of me.

Off Camera

"It's your brother!" Olivia skidded to a stop in front of me and Brynn. "I think he's hurt!"

I jumped up, sending my handful of playing cards flying all over the great room. "Where?"

"The yard. Ann and I were going out to the ice shed, and we were just in time to see the whole pile of firewood fall on his head," she said breathlessly as she led the way down the stairs to the back door. "He must have grabbed the wrong log and brought the pile down on himself."

That didn't sound like Frank. He's not a grab-some-random-log kind of guy. No, I realized grimly, if the woodpile had come down on Frank's head, someone else had made that happen.

We burst out into the yard. Frank was just sitting up and Ann was looking down at him with concern. He put a hand to his head, looking kind of woozy.

"What happened?" he mumbled as I reached his side.

"Don't move," I ordered. Glancing back at Olivia, I added, "Get the medics."

The medics who work on the show are real pros. They checked Frank over from head to toe. Aside from some scrapes and bruises and a big bump on the noggin, he was okay.

"You were lucky," the head medic told him as she packed up her stuff. "It could have been much worse."

"Yeah!" Bobby T exclaimed. Along with everyone else in the mansion, he'd come outside to rubberneck. "He could've been killed!"

One of the show's producers was sort of hovering around, watching. "Don't panic, everyone. No real harm done," he said, adjusting his power tie. "I'm sure it was just an accident, but one of the PAs is reviewing the tapes from the camera out there just to be sure."

At that moment Sylvia came running. "Bad news, boss," she said. "There's no footage."

"What do you mean, no footage?" The producer frowned. "The cameras are all still on."

Sylvia shrugged. "Yeah, it was on, but there's no picture. Must've been blocked or something."

"Where's the camera?" I was already scanning the area. There were several large trees that could be hiding the camera in question, along with the back of the ice shed. "Let's see if it's been disabled."

The producer hesitated. I guessed he didn't want to give away the location of the hidden camera. Then he glanced at Frank's bandaged forehead and shrugged.

"It's in the knothole in that tree over there." He pointed.

I gestured to James, who was standing with the others. "Give me a lift," I said.

James didn't seem too happy about the request. But he did it, hoisting me up so I could see the hidden camera.

"Here's the culprit." I reached in and pulled out a large, damp leaf.

"Dude, you're dripping on me," James complained. He let me drop to the ground a little harder than necessary.

I showed the leaf to the producer. "This was draped over the lens."

"Hmm." He didn't seem too concerned. "Must have blown over it. Bad luck."

I wasn't so sure luck had anything to do with it.

For one thing, the leaf was from a completely different kind of tree than the one where the camera was hidden.

When I glanced over at Frank, I forgot about all that for a moment. Brynn was kneeling beside him, brushing some dirt off his shirt.

"You poor thing," she said. "Are you sure you're okay?"

She picked a twig out of his dark hair. He blushed. And right then, for a tiny little fraction of a second, I entertained the idea that Frank might have done this on purpose to get Brynn's attention.

Nah. That had to be my paranoia talking. That wasn't Frank's style. He might be a woman-stealing jerk, but he wasn't that sneaky.

Kidding. Sort of.

Anyway, I pretended I wanted to help Frank clean himself up. We locked ourselves in the bathroom and discussed what had happened.

"Whoever did this is getting more serious," said Frank. "We need to step up our efforts before someone gets hurt." He winced and touched his bandaged head. "*Seriously* hurt, that is."

"Someone must've been hiding behind the woodpile," I said. "Maybe we can narrow down who it could have been. See who doesn't have an alibi."

We left the bathroom and split up. By asking around, we managed to account for almost everyone's whereabouts at the time. The only ones with no alibi were Mikey, Gail, and Mary. We eliminated Mary right away—not only had she been the prankster's latest target, but she was now terrified to go anywhere near the woodpile. Then there was Mikey. He said he'd been in the basement. As for Gail, she claimed she'd been taking a nap upstairs.

"Okay, we've already been watching Mikey," I said when Frank and I huddled again to compare notes. "But I'm thinking we should get serious about Gail as a suspect."

"Do you think she's strong enough to push over that woodpile?" Frank mused.

SUSPECT PROFILE

Name: Gail Digby

Hometown: St. Louis, Missouri

Physical description: 5'9", 145 lbs., sandy hair, brown eyes.

Occupation: High school student

Background: Oldest of three kids raised by single mother. Grew up in severe poverty.

Suspicious behavior: New round of pranks started at the same time she entered the mansion. No alibi for woodpile incident.

I shrugged. "Maybe. She's almost as tall as Ripley, and probably outweighs her."

"And all it would take is one good shove in the
right spot. Probably any guy in the house would
be strong enough, even Hal. Plus at least a few of
the girls—not just Gail and Ripley, but also Olivia
and maybe Ann."

It took me a moment to remember that Ann =
Silent Girl. "Right," I said. "So basically anyone but
Mary or Brynn."

Was I nuts, or did he actually wince when I said
Brynn's name? If so, he shook it off fast.

"I wish I'd been paying more attention to that
sound I heard," he said.

I nodded. "You said it sounded like a laugh."

"A little girl's laugh," Frank confirmed.

"Creepy." I thought about that story Veronica
had told us. The one about that director killing his
wife in front of their little girl.

But Frank's mind was going in another direction.

"Where was Ripley when it happened?" he asked. "You talked to her, right?"

"Yeah. She was in the kitchen with Hal. Why?"

He shrugged. "She was the one who sent me out there, remember?"

"True. But she was just passing the word on from Mary. Well, actually from Veronica, but you know what I mean." Call me slow, but it wasn't until I said it that I realized what he was driving at. "Oh! Do you think we should talk to Mary?"

"Couldn't hurt."

We found her washing dishes in the kitchen. When we asked her exactly what she'd told Ripley earlier, she looked confused. "What do you mean?" she said. "Veronica didn't give me any message. I haven't seen her all day."

"So you didn't tell Ripley to find someone to bring in more wood?" I asked.

She shook her head. "Why? Was I supposed to?"

"No, never mind." I looked at Frank. Now things were getting interesting. I wasn't about to cross Mikey or Gail or anyone else off the suspect list. Not yet.

But I was definitely going to be keeping an even closer eye on Ripley Lansing.

• • •

After dinner I hung out with Ripley for a while, listening to her talk about all the places she wanted to go shopping when she got out of the mansion. Frank was nowhere in sight. I hoped he was making more progress on the case than I was. I tried several times to change the subject to what was going on in the house. No dice. The girl loves talking about shopping.

Finally I couldn't take it anymore. I told Ripley I had to go. I'm not sure she even noticed when I left.

While looking for Frank, I came across Bobby T. He was in one of the parlors, staring intently at his laptop. His face was pale.

"Something wrong?" I asked. I suddenly realized that Frank and I hadn't talked much about Bobby T lately. For a while during the Mitch drama, we'd suspected Bobby of trying to drum up interesting episodes for his blog. Could he be behind the latest pranks? He liked to portray himself as an edgy kind of guy. And he certainly had the techie know-how to pull off some of the threats and stuff. But would he go so far as to hurt people?

He stared up at me, his eyes wide. "I was just checking the comments on my last blog entry," he said. "Take a look."

I leaned closer. He pointed to a particular message with a trembling finger.

Nice blog, Bobby, it read. *Maybe your friends and family can read from it at your funeral.*

"Whoa," I said. "Intense. When did that come in?"

"Not sure." Bobby still looked scared. "All the ID stuff has been scrubbed. I tried to trace the ISP, but no go."

I remembered something. The last two times threats had been sent by computer, everyone in the house had been on the "to" list.

"Can I check my e-mail?" I asked, reaching for the laptop.

Soon my in-box popped up on-screen. Sure enough, there was a new message from an unfamiliar sender. I clicked to open it.

You and your brother may have lived most of your lives apart, the message read. *But if you stay in this house, you'll die together.*

Planks a Million

"**A**ttention, please!" Veronica strode into the kitchen the next morning. Today her suit and shoes were dark brown. Her lipstick was still bright red. "I hope you all had a relaxing day yesterday. Because it's time for your next competition."

My heart sank. I'd hoped Joe and I might have a chance to talk after breakfast. The previous evening, he'd filled me in on the nastygrams he and Bobby had received. When I checked, one just like Joe's was waiting in my in-box. Everyone we'd asked so far had gotten similar messages.

But it seemed we would have to wait to investigate further. At least until after this challenge. Sometimes the most frustrating thing about being undercover is having to *stay* undercover. If you know what I mean.

Still, maybe part of me was a teensy bit relieved. I was feeling guilty because while Joe was checking e-mails with Bobby T, I'd been hanging out with Brynn. I was really starting to understand why Joe had wanted to spend every spare moment with her that first week. She was amazing in a way I couldn't quite describe. I really wasn't sure what to think about the way she made me feel. So I'd basically decided not to think about it at all.

The others were buzzing about Veronica's announcement. The host just smiled smugly for a moment, seeming to enjoy the suspense. Then she held up a hand for quiet.

"This one is called the Prissy Primpers Challenge," she announced.

James snorted with laughter. "Hear that, girls? You might actually be able to beat me in a contest with a name like that." He flexed his biceps. "Don't count on it, though."

"Don't laugh, James," Brynn teased. "Our challenge might be that we have to apply makeup to all the boys in the house."

"I hope so," said Hal. "That would actually be a nice change of pace from all the gross and scary challenges we've had so far."

Veronica looked amused. That wasn't a good sign.

"This one won't be scary, but I think you'll find it plenty gross," she said. "Follow me to the backyard, please."

When we got outside, we saw that the swimming pool had been filled with something—it looked like thick, multicolored goo. It smelled weird too, though I couldn't quite identify the scent. This time Veronica didn't keep us in suspense for long.

"The pool is full of a mix of every grooming product known to teenkind," she announced, stepping over to the edge of the pool. "Shampoo. Toothpaste. Hair gel. Pimple cream. Cologne of varying quality. Hair removal cream. Makeup. And the list goes on." She smirked. "Sounds tasty, no?"

"Sounds disgusting," Gail said.

Veronica didn't bother to respond to that. "You will be divided randomly into teams of four. One member of each team will have to balance on these."

She waved one red-manicured hand. Several PAs appeared on cue, each carrying a long, narrow wooden plank. They walked over and laid them out across the pool.

"Good thing that Sylvia chick doesn't have to do this part," Brynn whispered to me. "Those boards probably weigh more than she does." She shivered.

"Besides, I'm just glad she's not here. She makes me nervous."

I chuckled. On my other side, Joe shot me a suspicious look.

"Meanwhile," Veronica went on, "the other team members must scoop up the stuff in these." She stepped over to a box and pulled out several small fabric cases. For a second I wasn't sure what they were supposed to be.

"Are those makeup bags?" asked Olivia.

"Uh-huh," Ripley said. "They look like rip-offs of one my mom's company put out as a promotion. I have, like, three of them at home."

"Then perhaps you'll be good at this, Ms. Lansing," Veronica said. "As I was saying, you'll all need to scoop up as much of the substance as you can, using only your hands and these bags—no using your shoes or your shirts." She smirked. "And ladies, I certainly wouldn't recommend soaking it up with your hair. Not if you want to keep it, anyway." She strode toward a row of barrels a few yards away. "You'll want to fill your team's color-coded barrel as quickly as you can. Whichever team has the most in its barrel at the end wins."

"Sounds easy enough," said James, cracking his knuckles. "Let's do it!"

Veronica held up one very red finger in warning. "Not so fast, Mr. Sittenfeld," she said. "There's one more twist. If any of the people on the planks fall in, that person's team must stop collecting goo immediately." Her eyes twinkled with glee. "Plus, the person who falls in isn't allowed to shower or change clothes for the rest of the day."

"Oh, man," Bobby T muttered, reaching up and tugging on his blue hair. He was probably imagining it falling off in chunks—or at least coated with zit cream.

"Also, if any of the plank people choose to walk off voluntarily, their team will be out of the running entirely." Veronica smiled again. "Oh, but in the meantime, the plank standers *are* allowed to throw goo at the others to try to get them off. So can the rest of the team members. The only thing you can't do is touch the planks themselves." She chuckled evilly. "After all, that wouldn't be fair."

Next she announced the randomly chosen teams. First was the Red Team. That one included me, James, Olivia, and Brynn. The Blue Team consisted of Joe, Mikey, Mary, and Gail. And finally, there was the Green Team—Bobby T, Ripley, Hal, and Ann/Silent Girl.

"You should be on the plank," James said as soon as the teams were announced, pointing to

Olivia. "You look like you have good balance. And the rest of us will probably be faster with the bags."

"Hold on," Veronica said loudly. "Did I forget to mention that? *I* will decide which team members must stand on the planks."

It figured. After all, "life isn't fair" was pretty much the motto of this show.

Veronica chose Brynn for plank duty from our team. Brynn didn't look too happy about that. She glanced at the goo and grimaced.

Ripley looked even less happy when Veronica picked her for the Green Team. And the entire Blue Team groaned when the host named Mikey to hit the plank for them.

"*Stand* on the plank?" Mikey joked weakly. "I feel like I'm going to be *walking* the plank!"

James grinned. "Hope those planks are stronger than they look," he said. "Otherwise you're going to be smelling minty fresh, fat boy."

Veronica gave us a moment to huddle and strategize. "Listen, I have a plan," Olivia hissed at the rest of our team. She glanced suspiciously at the other two teams, obviously worried that they were going to eavesdrop on her brilliant idea.

"I have an idea, too," said James. "We kick butt and win. How's that for an idea?"

Olivia rolled her eyes. "No, listen," she urged. "I think we should start off throwing that slop at the other teams' plank people. If we can knock them both out early, we'll be able to win for sure!"

Brynn looked dubious. I knew how she felt. It didn't seem like much of a strategy.

But James grinned. "Knock fatso and Little Miss Rich Girl into that junk? I'm in. Let's do it!"

Then it was time for the plank people to take their positions. I felt even less confident about my team's game plan when I saw how precarious poor Brynn looked out there perched on the narrow plank. What if we missed and knocked her in by mistake?

But I didn't say anything. It was too late, anyway. The buzzer sounded, and the game was on.

The other teams started scooping and running. Olivia and James raced to the edge of the pool and started pelting the plank people with goo.

"Hey!" Mikey yelped as James hit him in the chest with his first handful. "Quit it!"

"Check it out!" Bobby T shouted, already returning from dumping his first bagful into a barrel. "They're going after Ripley! Two can play that game!"

He scooped up some goo and let it fly. Brynn let out a squeal of protest and tried to duck. But she wasn't fast enough.

SPLAT! The goo hit her square in the face. She bobbled, but didn't fall.

"Whoa, careful!" I cried, annoyed with Bobby. To retaliate, I grabbed some goo. It felt squishy and cold in my hand. I winged it at Bobby.

"Yo!" Bobby cried jumping aside just in time. "You're only supposed to throw it at the plank people!"

James laughed. "Hey, nobody said anything about that!" he crowed, slinging a handful of slop at Gail as she returned to the edge of the pool. He actually seemed to be enjoying this.

The whole pool area was a mess already. People from the other two teams were slipping and sliding in the ooze as they raced back and forth to their barrels.

"This isn't working!" Olivia cried, finally seeing the light. "Start filling the barrels!"

"Finally," I muttered. I scooped up some goo and ran toward the red barrel. Olivia was right behind me, though James was still back by the pool tossing goo at Ripley.

I reached the barrel first. It was big—as tall as my shoulders—and broad. I grabbed the edge and tipped my bag over it.

Then I did a double take. Oh no, not again . . .

"Hey!" I shouted, tossing my bag aside. "There's a body in here!"

Barreling Onward

SPLASH! Mikey lost his balance and fell into the pool of goo. That distracted everyone so much that nobody but me seemed to hear Frank's shout.

Everyone was laughing and pointing, including the other members of the Blue Team. I pushed past them all, racing to Frank's barrel. He already had it partly tipped on its side.

"What's going on?" A PA bustled over to us, looking annoyed. "What are you doing?"

"There's someone in there," Frank insisted. "A woman. We have to see if she's breathing."

"Nonsense." Veronica strode over, frowning. "What's this all about? I—" At that moment she looked inside the barrel and gasped. "Oh my God!" Spinning around, she made a slashing motion across her throat. "Cut! Cut the cameras!" she yelled.

I'm not sure anyone heard her. Mikey was just hauling himself out of the pool. Goo dripped from every inch of him. James was literally rolling on the ground with laughter.

Meanwhile, I was helping Frank tip the barrel the rest of the way over. Now I could see inside. The motionless figure of a woman was curled at the bottom.

"Isn't that the PA?" I said. "What was her name again?"

"Sylvia." Frank looked around urgently. "Hey! We need a medic over here!"

I crawled partway in. The barrel was deep, but I managed to grab her arm. It felt very cold, but I still checked carefully for a pulse.

"Stop the game!" I shouted, backing out quickly. "She's dead!"

That finally got everyone's attention. Soon the cameras were off and the place was swarming with producers, crew members, medics, and eventually police officers. We all stood around, staring, until Veronica came to her senses and chased us back into the house.

Frank and I stuck around out there as long as we

could. But we couldn't risk blowing our cover. We had to go inside with the others.

Inside, everyone was freaking out to various degrees. Brynn, Mary, Ann, and Olivia were sobbing. Bobby T looked awfully close to tears too. Gail, Mikey, Ripley, and James looked grim, and Hal just seemed confused. Maybe there's no such thing as murder on L-62.

"Dude, this is wacked," James announced to no one in particular as he paced around the great room.

"Oh my God, oh my God," mumbled Brynn. "I don't think I can take any more of this!"

"You might not have to," Ripley pointed out. "This could be it for *Deprivation House*."

Mikey nodded. He was sitting on the stone hearth of the fireplace, toweling the goo out of his hair. "With another death, the producers will probably just cancel the whole show."

"Maybe that's not such a bad thing." Bobby T's face was ashen. "I mean, I'm starting to wonder if maybe this house is cursed. You know, from that murder . . ."

Mary shuddered. "Don't talk about that," she begged. "It's too much! This is all too much!"

I had to agree with her there. "What do you think?" I murmured to Frank.

He shrugged. "We just have to wait and see what they tell us."

So that's what we did. Finally, after a seemingly endless wait of about an hour, Veronica came in. "I'm sure you're wondering what happened out there." She looked and sounded as composed as ever, though maybe not quite her usual twisted, coldhearted self. "First of all, I can tell you that this is *not* a repeat of the, er, previous situation. Sylvia was *not* murdered. She died of an aneurysm."

Frank and I exchanged a glance. An aneurysm? In a way it made perfect sense. Thinking back, the PA had been complaining about severe headaches all week. I was pretty sure that was a symptom. Still, it seemed like the world's craziest coincidence that she should happen to croak in the middle of one of our challenges.

"Really?" Frank spoke up. "I thought I saw a bump on her forehead."

Go Frank—I hadn't even noticed that. But Veronica nodded.

"She does have a lump," she said. "The medics figure she hit her head when she passed out and fell. The coroner should be able to confirm that."

"Wait." Mikey sounded bewildered. "You mean she had an aneurysm and fell into that barrel?"

For the first time, Veronica looked uncertain.

"We're not sure how she got in there yet," she admitted. "I probably shouldn't tell you this. . . ." She glanced toward the doors, as if hoping a producer would come in and rescue her. Then she shrugged and continued. "The police took one of the cameramen, Chuck, in for questioning. Apparently he's been providing Sylvia with nonprescription pain pills. Their theory is that he found her dead and panicked, thinking she OD'd. He could have stuffed her body into that barrel without realizing it would be used in a challenge so soon."

I was surprised she was telling us so much. Even though she looked calm, cool, and collected, with not a sleek blond hair out of place, I guessed she was as shaken up by this as anyone else.

I was even more surprised to realize what this meant: The game was still on. If the producers thought this was just terrible bad luck—sort of like Frank's "accident" with the log pile—they wouldn't shut us down. And why would they? They didn't know about the worst of what had happened since Mitch had left—the glass in the ice, Mary's attack, even the latest round of threatening e-mails. I bit my lip, wondering if it had been a huge mistake to keep that stuff from them.

"Wow," Bobby T said. "That's wild."

Olivia nodded. "It's sad that she died," she said.

"Still, at least it was sort of, you know, natural or whatever."

"And at least it wasn't some freaky little dead girl, either," Mary put in. Her eyes darted around to the shadowy corners of the huge room. "*This* time," she added softly.

Decisions, Decisions

Obviously, nobody was in the mood to continue the challenge. Instead, Veronica drew the name of a team out of a hat to decide the winner.

"Blue Team," she announced, glancing at the slip of paper. "That's Joe Carr, Mikey Chan, Mary Moore, and Gail Digby."

"Woo-hoo!" Mikey cheered weakly. When he pumped his fist, a little goo dripped off his shirt.

"So what do we win?" Gail asked.

"I'm glad you asked." Veronica's evil smile was creeping back. "Because this was a team challenge, *each* member of the winning team must choose a new deprivation for the entire house."

"What?" Mikey yelped. "You mean we're gonna lose four luxuries at once?"

"Oh, man," muttered Ripley.

Bobby T looked worried. "Remember, my fabulous Blue Team buds," he said, "having the Internet benefits all of us. Especially now that we don't have TV anymore."

"Good point," agreed Mikey, glaring briefly at me. Guess he was still holding that grudge.

"Oh, please." Gail rolled her eyes. "Plenty of people still live without the Internet every day, you know."

"Not by choice, I bet," Bobby retorted.

Veronica looked pleased. Probably because everyone else in the room was unhappy. Joe and the other Blue Teamers all looked kind of anxious at being stuck in this situation. And everyone else was already worrying about losing their favorite luxuries. Well, except maybe Gail. She probably wouldn't be happy until we were all living on bread and water in a bare room.

"All right, people." Veronica headed for the door. "Blue Team, I'll need your decisions in one hour."

"An hour?" Bobby cried in dismay. He gulped. "Um, I mean, that doesn't give them much time to think about this."

Or much time for him to come up with bribes, I

thought. He was really going to have to scramble if he had any hope of saving his blog access.

"One hour," Veronica repeated. "I'll see you then."

As soon as she left, everyone rushed the Blue Team members. I didn't want to get involved in all the lobbying myself.

Stepping over to Joe, I leaned toward him. "Try not to make too many enemies with this," I murmured in his ear. It was getting harder to stay under the radar when the two of us kept winning challenges.

Joe just looked at me and rolled his eyes. "Duh," he said.

O-o-okay. So maybe he didn't need my advice.

I headed for the door. I'd just stepped outside when I heard someone hurrying after me. It was Brynn.

"Hey," she said breathlessly. "It's a pretty crazy scene in there. I'm kind of glad our team didn't win."

"Me too," I agreed.

We wandered downstairs and out into the yard. The crew was already working on draining the pool. Yellow police tape marked out the area where we'd found Sylvia.

Luckily, the mansion's grounds were big enough

to avoid all that. We skirted around the hustle and bustle and headed for the wild area beyond the manicured yard. It was pretty cool back there. Ravines, rocky areas, scrubby brush. All kinds of wildlife. We scared up tons of birds, a jackrabbit, and a handful of lizards as we walked.

We wandered in silence for a while along the edge of the biggest ravine. Finally Brynn stopped and sat down on a wide, flat boulder. "I wonder if there are cameras way out here," she said, glancing around.

"I don't know. Maybe." I sat down on the same boulder. But I was careful to leave at least a foot of space between us. I admit it, I was feeling kind of self-conscious. I don't know if it was because we might be on camera, or if it was from being out there alone with Brynn.

Okay, scratch that. I *do* know which it was. It was being with Brynn. But possibly being on camera didn't help.

She was gazing back toward the house. From out here, it looked a lot smaller.

"I can't believe someone else died here," she said softly.

She looked so sad all of a sudden that I wanted to take her hand. But I didn't. Maybe it was those cameras. Or maybe I'm just a dork, like Joe always says.

"You heard what Veronica said," I told her. "It was just a freak thing. It could have happened anytime, anywhere."

"I know." She turned to face me, her huge green eyes scared and vulnerable. "But it happened *here*." She sighed. "You know, I kind of wish the show *had* been shut down by this, like those guys were saying. This was fun at first, but lately . . ." She smiled wanly. "Thirty thousand dollars is no million bucks, but at least it's something, right?"

I realized she was talking about dropping out again. "What?" I was horrified at the thought of losing her. Er, I mean, of the bad guy succeeding and driving away a deserving contestant. "No, Brynn," I blurted out. "You can't quit!"

She bit her lip. "I'm not usually a quitter. But things are so crazy around here." She stared at the bandages on her hands. "What if something worse happens next? I mean, I was the one who almost drank that glassy ice water, remember?"

I don't panic easily. But I was kind of panicking now. I flashed back to when Joe and I had received our instructions for this mission. The info had been hidden inside a fake book called *The Bonehead's Guide to Talking to Girls*. Right now, I kind of wished that book had been real. And that I'd memorized it.

"Listen." I leaned closer. "Whoever is doing this

stuff obviously wants us all to quit. You can't let them win. Besides . . ." I paused and swallowed hard. "I, uh, I can't imagine, you know, being in this house without you."

"Really?" Her smile lit up her face, chasing away the gloomy shadows from her eyes. "That's so sweet of you to say, Frank. I would miss you, too. You're really special, you know that? I mean it."

She leaned a tiny bit closer. I held my breath. For a second I thought . . .

But no. She glanced around and laughed. "It's weird, isn't it?" she said. "Never knowing if you're being filmed."

"Uh, yeah." I wiped my palms on my jeans. Even though it wasn't very hot out, they were kind of sweaty all of a sudden. "Should we head back to the house? Veronica will be coming for those decisions soon."

We returned to the great room to find everyone else still there. Joe shot us a suspicious glare. ATAC teaches us to be observant. I'm sure it hadn't escaped his attention that Brynn and I were the only ones missing.

Just then Veronica strode in. "Hello, everyone," she said. "I trust you have some decisions for me?"

Joe went first. "I choose to deprive the house of books and magazines."

He looked kind of smug when he said it. I could guess why. He knew getting rid of reading material would bug me more than anyone.

But I wasn't going to let it bother me. Actually, it was a pretty good choice. Nobody else looked particularly upset, except maybe Mary and Hal. And neither of them was likely to cause much trouble for us.

"I'll go next," Mikey spoke up.

"All right," Veronica said. "What's your decision, Mr. Chan?"

Mikey smiled. "I choose—exercise equipment."

"What?" James howled. "You can't do that!"

"Ah, but he can," said Veronica. "In fact, the crew is on its way to seal off the door right now."

For a second I thought James might leap across the room and throttle Mikey then and there. No wonder. He lives to work out. Plus everyone in the room knew that Mikey had done it to get back at him for all the "fatso" stuff.

Then it was Gail's turn. She chose to shut off the hot water taps in the bathrooms. There were a number of groans at that one.

Gail looked kind of smug. "I've had to live in apartments without hot water before. No big deal for me," she said. "We'll just see how the rest of you do when you have to live like poor folks, huh?"

"Don't worry." Veronica glanced pointedly at the walk-in fireplace. "You're all still welcome to heat up as much water as you like on the fire." She smirked. "Of course, you'll find that a bit more labor-intensive than turning a faucet."

"Great." Ripley rolled her eyes. "That'll really help when I want to take a shower."

Veronica turned to Mary, the final member of the Blue Team. "Ms. Moore, what about you?" she said. "Your decision, please."

Mary cleared her throat, looking nervous. "I, uh, I choose—Internet service," she stated meekly.

"Nooooo!" Bobby T cried. He leaped for his laptop, which was sitting on one of the coffee tables. He flipped it open and scrabbled at the keys. "I have to let my readers know. . . ."

He looked at the screen. Then his face crumpled. I actually felt kind of bad for the guy.

"Too late." Veronica smiled smugly. "You're already off-line."

Where There's Smoke . . .

I thought Bobby T was going to cry. He was staring at his Internet-less laptop as if someone just killed his best friend. Come to think of it, maybe someone had.

But that wasn't the end of the day's surprises. "You can start figuring out how to live with your new deprivations in a moment," Veronica announced. "First, I want to let you know there will be another elimination soon."

"Huh?" Olivia said. "But you said those would happen once a week. It hasn't been a week since the last one."

Veronica did *not* look sympathetic. "Life doesn't always happen on schedule," she said. "Not even in

125

Deprivation House." She turned as if to leave, then paused. "Oh, one more thing." She smiled. "Actually, *two* more things. George and Georgina, come on in!"

The door opened. A pair of teenagers walked in, a guy and a girl. They were both blond. They also shared the same round blue eyes, full cheeks, and button noses.

"Please say hello to George and Georgina Taggart," Veronica said. "They're twins, and they'll both be joining you here in the mansion."

"Hey," George said with a grin. "What's up?"

Georgina rolled her eyes. "Have some class, George," she complained. "You sound like a hood."

"Nice," murmured Gail sarcastically.

Frank was standing nearby. I stepped toward him. "Check it out," I whispered. "Georgina looks a lot like Brynn. How about you go for her and leave Brynn to me?"

I was joking. Sort of. Frank looked irritated and didn't say anything.

"All right, then." Veronica seemed pleased now that just about everybody was in a state of shock and/or dismay. "I'll leave you to get acquainted. For now."

She left. Georgina glanced around. "Hi," she said, stepping toward Brynn. "Cute sweater. We look like the same size—I might want to borrow that some-time."

Brynn looked taken aback. "Oh," she stammered. "Um, sure."

Someone let out a groan. It was Bobby T. I doubt he'd even noticed the new arrivals. He was still staring at his laptop.

"It'll be okay, dude," James told him. "This just means you'll have to interact with real live people instead of virtual ones."

Bobby didn't look amused. He stood and tucked his laptop under his arm. "I think I'll go take a nap," he announced with a frown. "What else is there to do in this place now?"

He stomped off and disappeared through the door. George Taggart stared after him curiously.

"What's with him?" he asked.

Ripley rolled her eyes. "Never mind," she said. "So, where are you two from?"

I left her to play welcome wagon. Brynn had drifted over to stand beside Frank again. The two of them were leaning toward each other, talking quietly.

"Hey," I said, stepping over to them. "Bro. Want to go outside for some fresh air?"

"Can I come too?" Brynn asked before Frank could answer. She shrugged apologetically. "I just don't want to be alone right now. You know."

I didn't bother to point out that there were a dozen other people in the mansion she could be not-alone with. Why did it have to be Frank? Her sudden interest in my brother was getting really annoying.

"Never mind," I muttered. "Actually, I think I'll stick around and meet the newbies."

Everyone except Bobby hung out for a while getting acquainted or talking about everything that had happened that day. But eventually people started to drift off. Ripley and Olivia took the twins for a tour of the rest of the mansion. James went out to chop wood—probably the closest he could come to a workout. Others just wandered away without explanation.

Finally the only ones left in the great room were me, Frank, Brynn, Silent Girl, and Hal. Brynn and Frank were sitting together on the couch. They were mostly talking about nothing. Hal was scribbling notes on his pad, his mind probably light-years away. Silent Girl was just sitting there staring at the fire. Silently.

I stood up. "I'm hungry," I announced. "Think I'll grab a snack."

Brynn was the only one who looked up. "See you," she said with a smile.

I wandered out, trying not to think about leaving her there with Frank. Instead I thought about the mission. Now that someone else had died, things seemed much more urgent. Had Sylvia really died of an aneurysm? Or could someone in the house want that prize money enough to kill for it?

In a way, it made no sense. What if the whole show had been shut down? Then nobody would get that million-dollar prize. What would anyone have to gain by that?

Since we seemed to have a little downtime, I decided to snoop around a bit. Maybe I could get some more info on our prime suspects.

First I checked on Bobby T. When I peeked into his room, he was sprawled out on the bed. He appeared to be sound asleep.

I moved on. Just down the hall was the bedroom shared by three of the girls, including Ripley and Gail.

When I peeked in through the half-open door, neither of them were in there. But the third roomie was—Mary. Her back was to the door, and she was doing some kind of weird headstand. It looked like yoga to me, though I'm no expert on that stuff.

Whoa. Who knew there was such a tight little body under those baggy dresses she always wore? Also, I couldn't help wondering if yoga was a regular part of her homeschool curriculum, because she was doing some pretty intense-looking moves. She started off doing a headstand, but then she lifted herself up until her head was off the floor and she was balancing only on her forearms as she moved her legs around in different poses. Who says skinny little girls can't have upper-body strength?

I only watched for a second before I started to feel like a Peeping Tom. She was showing almost as much skin as Ripley always did. I left her to it and moved on, still keeping a lookout for our major suspects.

Nobody else was upstairs. As I headed down to the first floor, I noticed Mikey. He was standing by the back door looking furtive. A moment later he ducked outside.

I was pretty sure he hadn't seen me. What was he up to? I decided to find out if I could.

Dashing for the door, I followed him outside. He was halfway across the yard, heading toward the ice shed. He had to take the long way around the police tape near the pool.

I started to follow. But just then a voice called my name. I turned to see Ripley hurrying toward me.

"Hey," she greeted me. "How about those Taggart twins? They seem really full of themselves."

"Oh yeah?" I shrugged, a little distracted. Mikey

had just disappeared around the corner of the shed. "You seemed to be getting along with them pretty well earlier."

She laughed. "Oh, trust me," she said. "When you grow up in the spotlight, you learn to get along with everyone."

I didn't bother to point out that she hadn't learned that lesson too well. Wasn't that why she was here? To prove that she *could* get along without acting like a spoiled brat?

"Anyway, it's crazy how this show keeps throwing these surprises at us," she went on. "I can't believe we got two new people *and* four new deprivations on the same day."

"Don't forget the elimination," I said. "Sounds like that could happen today too."

"Good point." She adjusted her hat. "Who do you think will get axed? I'm guessing Bobby, thanks to that little tantrum just now."

"Yeah, could be." I was still distracted. But this time it wasn't because of Mikey. "Hey, do you smell smoke?"

"Yeah." She sniffed the air, not seeming very interested. "Probably just the chimney. Or maybe it's the ghost of that Sylvia woman—she must have smoked about five packs a day."

I took a step back toward the house, trying to

locate the source of the smoke. It didn't smell like cigarettes. It didn't really smell like woodsmoke, either.

Glancing up, I saw a tendril of smoke snaking out from one of the windows. "Hey!" I cried. "I think it's coming from one of the bedrooms upstairs!"

Without waiting for an answer, I raced toward the nearest second-story balcony. With a running start, I was able to jump up and grab the metal supports underneath it. Then I swung myself up and over the railing.

"What are you doing?" Ripley sounded perplexed.

I didn't stop to answer. The smell of smoke was stronger up here. Much stronger.

I crossed the balcony in one jump. The door was locked, so I peered in the window.

It was Bobby T's bedroom. The room was full of smoke. Bobby was still in there, asleep—only now he was lying in a bed of flame!

Red-hot and Red-handed

Brynn and I were walking through the foyer when I heard muffled shouts from upstairs. It sounded like Joe.

I sprinted for the steps. Halfway up, I smelled smoke. That got me moving even faster.

The shouts were coming from the room I shared with Bobby T and Hal. I burst in just in time to hear the crash of breaking glass. A second later Joe tumbled in through the window.

"Fire!" he shouted hoarsely.

"Aaaah!" Bobby was lying on the big double bed, totally surrounded by fire. He sat up, looking terrified. "What's happening?"

There was a line of flame all around the outside

edge of the mattress. "Get him out of there!" I shouted to Joe. I was already racing back into the hall. A fire extinguisher was hanging out there.

By the time I got back, Bobby was leaning against the wall near the door. Joe was nearby, beating out a few sparks trying to take hold on his own shirt. Both of them seemed to be okay.

"Stand back!" I called. Then I let the fire extinguisher rip. Thick foam shot out, quickly suppressing the fire.

When the hissing noise stopped, I heard cries and running footsteps from the hall. A second later most of our housemates burst in, soon followed by Veronica and several crew members.

"What's going on in here?" the host exclaimed. She stopped short when she saw the singed and foam-soaked bed. "Oh!"

There was a burst of chatter. But Bobby's voice cut through it like a knife.

"That's it!" he said loudly. "I want out!"

"Huh?" One of the crew guys turned to him. "Of course we'll get you a new bed, but if you'd rather move into a different bedroom, I suppose—"

"No, I mean I've had enough." Bobby looked grim. "I'm going to take the money and run. I still get thirty thou, right?"

"Oh, Bobby," Ripley exclaimed. "Are you really going to quit?"

"Yes," Veronica added. "Are you sure about this? I'll give you one chance to change your mind, considering the circumstances, but—"

"I'm not changing my mind," Bobby interrupted. "I'm out of here. This isn't worth a few extra blog hits." He grabbed his laptop from the bedside table, where it had miraculously escaped the fire and foam. "Especially since I can't even blog anymore."

Veronica shrugged. "Then it's official. Pack your things, and someone will call you a cab."

Bobby didn't have much to say as he grabbed the rest of his stuff. Within minutes, he was gone.

The producers seemed worried now. Not only had someone disabled the smoke alarm, but the room's automated camera as well. A shirt had been draped over the lens. In fact, it was one of my shirts. Definitely suspicious.

They shut off all the cameras—actually telling us they were doing it this time—and then brought us all into the great room for a serious talk.

"We will be investigating the cause of this fire," the head producer guy said sternly. "In the meantime, we're getting very concerned about all the things that have gone wrong lately. In fact, we're seriously considering shutting down the production."

"No way!" James burst out. "Dude, you can't do that. Not when I can almost taste the million!"

"Yeah," Georgina spoke up. "And I just got here!"

Olivia nodded. "Besides, Bobby probably started that fire himself. That way he had an out—a way to quit without looking like a coward." She shrugged and glanced around the room. "Not to mention a way to go out with a bang for his blog, especially now that he can't blog from the house anymore."

The producer looked uncertain. I wondered what he was thinking. Based on the comments on Bobby's blog, the show was already getting tons of buzz, even though it hadn't started airing yet. The producers probably hated the thought of pulling the plug on a potential hit.

"That's an interesting theory," the producer said to Olivia. "We'll take it under advisement. I suppose for now you should all just go about your business here."

"Woo-hoo!" James pumped his fist. "The show must go on."

Veronica shot him a disgusted look. So did several others.

Joe and I needed to talk. And soon. I waited until Brynn was busy talking with the twins, then slipped away to the supply closet.

Joe joined me there a few minutes later. "So what do you think of Olivia's theory?" he asked immediately.

"It makes a lot of sense, logically speaking." I shrugged. "But I just don't know if I believe it. I keep remembering the look of raw terror on Bobby's face when he woke up."

"Yeah." It looked like Joe remembered too. "So then who set that fire?"

I shook my head. "That's the question of the hour. It could have been anyone."

"Not anyone," he reminded me. "Whoever did it must have sneaked up there while we were in the kitchen. That means it wasn't us, or Brynn. . . ."

"Or Hal or Ann," I continued.

"Or Ripley," added Joe. "She was outside with me when I smelled the smoke. She caught up with me when I was trying to follow . . ." His words trailed off, and he gasped.

"What?" I demanded.

"Mikey," he said. "I saw him acting weird—like he was nervous. He went sneaking out of the house, and I tried to follow him. But Ripley waylaid me."

"Interesting. So you think he could've set the fire?"

"Maybe. I'd looked in on Bobby and he was fine. But I was down the hall for a few minutes after that.

It might have been enough time for Mikey to sneak in and start the fire."

"Okay," I said. "We'd better try to question Mikey about this. But I also can't help thinking about Gail."

Joe nodded. "Because of the arson thing, you mean?"

"They say the apple doesn't fall far from the tree, right?"

Before either of us could say anything else, we heard Veronica on the intercom system, calling everyone back to the great room. "Uh-oh," Joe said. "Either something else happened . . ."

"Or it's elimination time," I finished. My stomach twisted nervously. Joe and I were deep undercover—Veronica and the other judges had no idea who we really were or why we were really on the show. If they decided to kick us off, there was nothing we could do about it.

Soon everyone was gathered around the fireplace. "I won't keep you in suspense," Veronica said. "The other judges and I have reviewed the tapes since the last elimination. Our decision is unanimous. The next person to go will be . . ."

Despite her promise not to keep us in suspense, she paused. Her eyes wandered over us, each person in turn. When those pitiless eyes met mine, I did my best not to shiver. You could have heard a pin drop.

"The next person to go," she said again, "will be—Mikey Chan."

My eyebrows shot up. I guess others were surprised too. There was a lot of murmuring.

Mikey's eyes went wide, and his round face turned red. "But I—I—," he stammered.

Veronica didn't let him finish. "The camera sees everything, Mikey," she said. "Take a look."

She waved a hand, and a PA rolled in a large TV set. Images flashed on the screen. Images of Mikey tiptoeing into the supply closet—the bathroom—the ice shed. Then an image of him tossing something into the fireplace.

I leaned forward. "What was that?"

"Candy bar wrappers," Veronica replied. She smiled her icy smile. "Our Mikey has been sneaking junk food all week long—actually, ever since junk food got taken away. He got the stuff from our old friend Mitch and has been hoarding it."

"But—," Mikey sputtered.

"We've been aware of it all along, of course," Veronica went on. "However, we chose not to address it. Until now." She turned toward Mikey. "Mikey Chan, you have deprived yourself of the chance to be a millionaire."

"But it's not fair!" Mikey burst out, looking close to tears. "If you're going to kick me out for that, Ripley should go too! She's been doing the same thing—she ate stuff during her punishment when she was supposed to have only bread and water!"

"What?" cried Ripley. "I don't know what he's talking about!"

"I saw you!" Mikey pointed to her. "You were eating in the Deprivation Chamber. I know it."

James laughed. "Yeah, right," he said. "Okay, so we have Ripley." He moved his hands up and down close together to indicate a sort of curvy stick figure. "And then we have you." This time he spread his hands far apart, tracing out a shape closer to a beach ball. "Which of these two has been sneaking extra food?"

A few people laughed. Even Veronica cracked a smile—a small one. "Don't make yourself look worse, Mikey," she advised. "I'll have to ask you to pack your things and leave. Now."

Joe and I had to stand there in front of the cameras with the others while Mikey took his walk of shame. But as soon as that was over, we met up in the bathroom.

"Guess this explains all those times we surprised Mikey in the supply closet or saw him sneaking around," Joe said.

"True," I agreed. "But that doesn't mean he wasn't our culprit."

Joe shrugged. "Guess we'll find out. If nothing else happens, we'll know it was him."

We didn't have long to wait. Everyone was eating dinner when Olivia excused herself to go to the bathroom. A moment later a scream rang out.

When we all got there, she was standing in the bathroom doorway staring at the floor. Someone had written a message on the tile in thick black letters: TWO MORE DOWN, A DOZEN TO GO. WILL **YOU** BE THE NEXT VICTIM?

Rattled

Okay, so it hadn't been Mikey. We got that, loud and clear.

I wondered if this would finally be the last straw for the producers. I was expecting Veronica to burst in and announce that the show was over. But I guess the cameras were off, because nobody turned up.

Frank was already on his knees, examining the scrawled message. "I think this is written in eyeliner." He held up his fingers. They were smudged with black.

Ripley let out a pained little shriek. "It *is*!" she cried, leaping over to grab a tube lying on the floor nearby. "It's *my* eyeliner!" She waved the tube around, looking upset. "Do you guys know how much this stuff costs? It's ruined!"

Olivia shot her a suspicious look. "Interesting," she said. "First someone writes a message using your lipstick, then another one turns up with your eyeliner. Almost seems like a pattern, doesn't it?"

Ripley tossed the empty tube aside and planted her hands on her hips. "Are you accusing me of something?"

"No." Olivia shrugged. "Just making an observation."

Meanwhile Georgina was looking freaked out. "What is this place, anyway?" she exclaimed. "Is this all part of the show?"

"Not exactly . . ." Brynn started filling her in, with help from Hal and James.

Meanwhile, Gail and Olivia were still staring at Ripley. "Okay, now what Mikey said about you sneaking around is sort of making sense," Olivia said.

"Yeah. I always wondered why someone like you would come on a show like this," said Gail. "It's not like you need the money. Are you a ringer or something?"

"What do you mean?" Ripley looked confused. Maybe she didn't know what a ringer was. Or maybe she just assumed everyone knew why she was really there.

"She means you could be working for the show," Olivia explained. "Doing all this weird stuff to try to freak us out. Hysterical contestants equal bigger ratings, right?"

You had to hand it to Olivia. The girl was a quick thinker. Logical, too. Although she was forgetting a few key points.

"Are you nuts?" James put in. "Yeah, maybe the producers might try to psych us out by sending stupid messages and stuff. But they wouldn't do this." He opened his mouth and pointed inside. It still looked raw and red from his encounter with the glassy ice. "Or that." He pointed at Brynn's bandaged hands. "They wouldn't even do something like push her down." He glanced at Mary, then shrugged. "Of course, that could've just been a passing breeze."

I hid a smile as I flashed to the image of Mary in those tough yoga poses. James had better hope she never got fed up with him teasing her about being skinny and weak. She was probably a whole lot stronger than he realized.

Olivia was still glaring at Ripley. "Mikey might've been a pig," she said. "But I don't think he was a liar. So why did he say that about you eating during your punishment?"

Ripley frowned. Then she sighed. "Fine," she said. "You want the truth?"

"That would be nice," Gail retorted.

I glanced at Frank. He looked as confused as I felt.

"I'm not in cahoots with the producers," Ripley said. "I swear. The only thing is . . . I have a sort of, um, eating disorder."

One or two people gasped. Others looked unsurprised.

"Wow," said Olivia. "Too bad Bobby left. He would've loved to put that kind of scoop on his blog."

Ripley ignored the comment. "Anyway, my parents said I could only be on the show if the staff kept an eye on me. You know, foodwise. Since it was for a medical reason, the producers agreed." She shrugged. "So when I lost that challenge, they sneaked me some food anyway."

"So you *were* cheating!" Gail sounded outraged. "Figures the rich girl would figure out a way around things."

"But I wasn't!" Ripley protested. "Not really. See, they took away my straightening iron as a secret alternative punishment." She tugged on her wavy hair. "Trust me, having to walk around like this is *way* worse than the food thing."

"If you say so." James rolled his eyes. "I'd rather

shave my head and go naked than get stuck with bread and water."

"Anyway, I'm sorry I couldn't tell you before," Ripley said. "But I hope this convinces you that I'm definitely not the one who did this." She waved a hand at the eyeliner message. "Or any of the other weird stuff that's been happening. Nope, I didn't do the ice thing, or dump that firewood on Frank, or knock Mary down." She crossed her arms and glanced around the room. "But I'm pretty sure I know who *did* do it all."

"Huh?" said Frank, looking startled.

I knew how he felt. It was going to be really embarrassing if we got scooped on our mission by some L.A. socialite.

"Who did it?" Olivia demanded.

Ripley shook her head. "I'm no snitch," she said. "I'm not going to tell—for now, anyway. But if anything else happens, or I find out that Sylvia woman's death wasn't an accident, I'll go straight to the producers with what I know. Consider yourself warned."

I sidled toward Frank. "We should talk," I muttered.

"Yeah. Outside?"

I nodded. Since the cameras didn't seem to be on, it didn't much matter where we went. "Meet you there in five."

It was a good fifteen minutes before Frank showed up. I spent the extra time pacing around the yard, trying to figure out what all this meant. Only one thing seemed certain—whoever was doing the bad stuff was definitely still in the mansion.

When Frank finally appeared, I glanced at my watch. "Glad you could make it," I said.

"I got here as fast as I could," he retorted. "It took a while to lose Brynn."

That was so not what I wanted to hear. "I bet," I said sarcastically. "What, did she finally excuse herself to wipe off your drool?"

"Grow up, Joe," he muttered. "We don't have time for this right now."

That put me over the edge. "Oh yeah?" I demanded. "When *will* we have time to talk about how you stole her right out from under me? Huh? Because I'd like to put it on my schedule."

He scowled at me. I scowled back at him. Then, after a moment, his shoulders slumped.

"Look," he said, all the anger gone from his voice. "This is getting stupid, and more importantly, it's getting in the way. So you know what? You're right. You saw Brynn first. You—you should have her. I won't stand in your way anymore, I swear."

"Good," I said. "That's more like it."

He didn't say anything else. I peered at him. He

looked kind of upset. Not upset as in, Joe-won-and-I'm-a-loser upset. More like *upset* upset.

"Hold the phone," I said. "What's with you?"

"What do you mean? Nothing. I'm just thinking about the mission."

"Don't give me that. This is me you're talking to." I reached over and gave him a shove. "You don't have, like, real feelings for Brynn, do you?"

"No," he said quickly.

Too quickly. That told me all I needed to know. My eyes widened, and I smiled. "Oh, man, you so totally *do*!" I cried in amazement. "Dude! You really *like* this girl, don't you?"

His face was going bright red. "Drop it, Joe," he mumbled.

I couldn't believe it. Frank, good old scared-of-girls Frank, had actually fallen for Brynn. Who could have guessed? Leave it to good-guy Frank to offer to sacrifice all that for the sake of the mission. What a dork!

Obviously this changed everything. Sure, I dug Brynn. She was cute, she was fun to hang out with, and she was an awesome way to spend the down-time in the mansion. But I wasn't about to propose or anything. If Frank was really falling for her, there was only one thing to do.

I smacked him on the shoulder. "It's okay, bro.

I'm the one who's gonna back off." I grinned at him. "But only if you swear not to chicken out on this! You gotta tell her how you feel."

"What?" He looked alarmed. "Uh, I don't think so."

"Come on, man! She likes you, too. Just do that Mr. Good Guy honest thing you do, and she'll be all over you."

He shook his head and kicked at the grass. "What's the point? I can't be honest with her even if I wanted to. Undercover, remember? She doesn't even know my real name. And she's such an honest person herself, she'd never understand. . . ." He shook his head, looking pained. "Anyway, we shouldn't be wasting time on this. We're here to work, remember?"

He sounded kind of bummed out. Not to mention way uncomfortable with the whole Brynn line of conversation. I decided to take pity on him and let him change the subject.

"Okay," I said. "So what do you think of Ripley's big announcement?"

He looked relieved. "Interesting," he replied. "I don't think it lets her off the hook, though. She could be covering her own tracks by claiming to know who it is."

"You're right. Should we try to question her?"

"Definitely. But not right now—I passed her on

my way out and she was just heading into the bathroom to take a shower."

I nodded. "If she *does* actually know who's been doing the stuff, who do you think it could be? Gail?"

"That would make sense. They're roommates. And they don't get along very well. Should we go talk to her while we're waiting for Ripley to get out of the shower?"

"Exactly what I was going to suggest." I grinned at him, suddenly very glad that we'd cleared the air about the Brynn thing. I hadn't realized until that moment just how tense things had been between us the past few days.

"Let's just go over the facts one more time before we head in." Frank had that look on his face that said his mind was clicking along at a million miles per hour. "One thing bothers me about Gail and Ripley as suspects. Is either of them physically capable of some of the stuff we're talking about? Like knocking over the woodpile—or knocking out Sylvia, if that turns out to be connected?"

I shrugged, a little impatient. Frank is always looking to dot all our i's and cross our t's. I'm more of an immediate-action kind of guy.

"We already talked about that," I reminded him. "Ripley's thin, but she's fit. She's mentioned a few times having a personal trainer back home. And

Gail is no lightweight; I think she's got bigger guns than I do."

"Okay," said Frank. "So we think most of the guys and the fitter, stronger girls are capable of that stuff? Say, everyone except maybe Hal, Brynn, Ann, Olivia, and Mary?"

"Well, I'd say Olivia and Hal are marginal, but—oh!" Suddenly I remembered something. "We can probably cross Mary off the weaklings list too."

"What do you mean? She's the smallest person here."

"I know. But maybe not the weakest . . ." I told him about seeing her doing yoga in her room. "So she's obviously not as feeble as we thought."

"Interesting." Frank looked thoughtful. "So quiet little Mary isn't what she seems. It could be strategy—and if so, that shows she's a lot more competitive than we've been assuming. Maybe even competitive enough to try to scare other people away?"

I couldn't help being dubious. "I guess anything's possible. Maybe we should think about her more if Ripley and Gail don't pan out."

"Agreed." Frank nodded. "For now, let's see if we can find Gail."

She wasn't in the kitchen, Deprivation Chamber, or great room. And her bedroom was deserted. The sound of the running shower came faintly from the direction of the girls' bathroom.

"How can Ripley stand that cold water for so long?" The closest bed was rumpled, the covers mounded up in the middle. I flopped down on it, figuring whoever it belonged to wouldn't mind—if she even noticed I'd been there. "You don't think secret hot water was part of her deal with the producers too, do you?"

Frank didn't seem to be listening. He stepped over to one of the dressers. "You know, maybe we should take a look around," he said, sliding open one of the drawers. "Considering a couple of our prime suspects are staying in this room."

"Good plan. I—Ow!" I cried as a sudden jab sent a spurt of fire through my thigh.

Frank glanced over. "What's the matter?"

I flipped back the covers—and froze. A large snake was staring back at me. Its tail flicked, and I heard an ominous rattling sound.

Under the Radar

"**G**et back, Joe!" I shouted. Grabbing a large bath towel off the dresser, I flung it over the snake. It hissed and rattled angrily. But the towel disabled it long enough for Joe to roll off the bed, clutching his leg.

I sprang for the intercom on the wall. "Medic!" I shouted into it. "We have a snakebite situation on the second floor. Hurry!"

The snake was slithering out from under the towel by now. I grabbed a plastic wastebasket and slammed it down, trapping it. Its tail thudded furiously against the inside.

Joe was writhing on the floor in pain. "Don't just stand there!" he choked out. "Someone put that thing here! If you hurry . . ."

I hesitated. He was right—whoever had planted that snake couldn't have gotten far. But I didn't want to leave Joe. Not to mention the fact that I wasn't about to let go of that wastebasket . . .

At that moment Ripley appeared in the doorway, wrapped in a towel. "Hey," she said. "What are you guys doing in here?" She blinked at Joe. "And what's with him? Is he having a seizure?"

"She can hold it," Joe gasped out. "Go! Before it's too late!"

In the distance, I could hear shouts—that had to be the medics. "Come over here," I told Ripley. "Hold this wastebasket right where it is—don't let go."

I guess I sounded like I knew what I was doing, because she obeyed.

"Why can't I let go?" she asked.

I was already racing for the door. "If you do, the snake will get loose," I called back over my shoulder.

She let out a shriek. "Snake?"

I didn't stick around to explain. Joe would have to handle that.

Sprinting down the hallway, I checked out the nearby rooms. All empty. Downstairs, I was just in time to see Gail and Olivia coming out of the

Deprivation Chamber. Veronica was standing outside watching them.

Deciding that made them poor suspects for the snake thing, I kept going. I was heading for the kitchen when I happened to glance out through the back door. Someone was out there.

Veering that way, I burst outside to find Mary peeling off a pair of heavy leather gloves. She looked startled by my sudden arrival.

"Mary," I blurted out in surprise. "So it's true—you really can handle a rattler!"

I know, I know. That was stupid. She knew right away that I was onto her. Tossing the gloves aside, she sprinted across the yard.

It turned out she wasn't just stronger than she looked. She was faster, too. Even dressed in one of her frumpy long skirts. I chased her, but she kept ahead of me all the way across the yard and through the rocky, scrubby area beyond.

She was heading straight for the edge of the biggest ravine. And she wasn't slowing down. That gave me the extra burst of speed I needed. I tackled her just a few feet from the drop-off.

"No!" she screamed. "Let me go! I didn't do anything."

I guess all the action and shouting had attracted

attention. James and the new kid, George, came running up behind us.

"What's going on?" James exclaimed. "Frank, dude, if that's how you always try to get girls . . ."

"Shut up," I told him. It wasn't easy holding on to Mary. She was wriggling like a cat. A cat with sharp claws. I winced as her fingernails scraped my arm. "It's been Mary all along. She's the one who did all that stuff—now help me get her back to the house."

SUSPECT PROFILE

Name: Mary Moore

Hometown: Rural Georgia

Physical description: 5'2", 105 lbs., brown hair, brown eyes. Drab, old-fashioned, modest dress.

Occupation: Home-schooled student.

Background: The oldest of five kids from a poor family. Not many other details known.

Suspicious behavior: Flew so far under the radar she was practically invisible.

Suspected of: Everything that Mitch didn't do.

Possible motive: One million dollars.

"Are you sure you're okay?" Brynn asked anxiously.

Joe nodded. "I'll be fine," he told her. Shooting me a sly look, he added, "Thanks to my incredibly brave brother, that is. He's quite a guy, isn't he?"

I felt my face go red. Subtle, Joe. Real subtle.

Brynn hurried over and squeezed my arm. "He sure is," she said. "You *are* brave, Frank. Smart, too. Who could've guessed sweet little Mary was behind all the trouble all along?"

Who indeed. My gaze wandered toward Mary. She was standing near the fireplace a few yards away, sort of slumped and defeated-looking. She was handcuffed, and the cops were talking to Veronica and some of the producers nearby.

"I still don't understand," Olivia complained. Things had been chaotic for a while. But by now, everyone in the house was clustered in the great room watching the proceedings. "So if Mary confessed to the snake and all that other stuff, then who pushed her down that night?"

"Nobody," I replied. "She made up that whole story about seeing the little girl, and she just rolled in the mud to make it believable." That wasn't all she'd confessed to. Once she'd realized she was busted, Mary had also admitted to sending those threatening letters and e-mails, planting that dead bird, writing on Ripley's face and on the bathroom floor, and pushing over the woodpile on me. Joe and I hadn't been able to hear all of it—Veronica and the cops kept chasing us away.

"What a freak," Gail declared loudly, glaring over at Mary. "So does this mean she killed that PA woman, too?"

At that, Mary's head snapped up. Guess she'd been listening.

"I didn't kill anybody, I swear!" she cried. "She just died. I wasn't trying to hurt anyone. I just wanted to—to win."

"So you're saying you didn't have anything to do with Sylvia ending up in that barrel?" Olivia challenged.

Mary blinked rapidly. She glanced around at all of us, looking like a trapped animal. Then she let out a wail that made us all jump in surprise.

"But I'm telling you, I didn't kill her!" she cried. "I—I just knocked her over the head with a piece of wood. Not even that hard."

"She could be telling the truth," Hal spoke up. "The stress of getting knocked out and everything might've brought on the aneurysm. And that Sylvia had all sorts of risk factors going on—smoking, high-stress job, tense personality . . ." At everyone's looks of surprise, he shrugged. "I've been researching which medical conditions might be the leading causes of death on L-62."

"Anyway, I only did it because she was about to catch me in the supply room when I was going to switch out all the salt and sugar." Mary bit her lip so hard I was afraid she'd draw blood. Her moment of drama had passed, and she was back to looking defeated again. "I knew she'd tell everyone she saw me down there."

"Switching salt and sugar?" Olivia sounded skeptical. "Okay, so how do you go from lame pranks like that to trying to kill Joe with a rattlesnake?"

Mary stared down at the floor. "I panicked then, too," she admitted. "The snake was meant to scare Ripley. I thought she was about to tattle on me."

"Oh my God." Ripley rolled her eyes. "I was totally bluffing! I had no clue who did any of that stuff."

"Just goes to show, princess, it doesn't pay to lie. Not even for rich girls," James said with a snort. Then he glared at Mary. "But hey, Miss I-Didn't-Want-to-Hurt-Anyone, what about that freaking ice trick of yours? That could've killed someone—namely, me!"

"And what about those knives that cut Brynn?" Ripley added. "Or the fire in Bobby's room?"

Mary shook her head vigorously. "I didn't have

anything to do with any of that!" By now, tears were flowing freely down her cheeks. "I swear!"

It was tough not to be skeptical. Mary hadn't exactly shown herself to be trustworthy. Judging by the looks on the faces around me, I wasn't the only one who felt that way. At the same time, I had a nagging feeling—something didn't feel quite right to me about Mary having been behind all of this. She was clearly unbalanced, and got scared easily. But was she capable of premeditated violent acts? After all, why would Mary confess to some, but not *all* of the acts if she was, in fact, responsible for all of them? Or were Joe and I still missing something here?

"Come along, miss." A police officer appeared and took Mary by the arm. "Let's get you down to the station. Your parents will be flying in as soon as possible."

As soon as Mary and the police were gone, everyone else went back to buzzing about what had happened. A few people wandered away to the bathroom or wherever. Meanwhile Joe and I drifted off to a private corner of the great room.

"So what do you think?" Joe murmured, glancing around to make sure we wouldn't be overheard by the others. Neither of us was too concerned about the cameras at the moment—I seriously doubted the producers were going to be airing any of today's events. "If my math is right, there's still some voluntary dropout money left. Twenty grand to the next guy who leaves, and ten K after that. That's thirty large between the two of us."

"You know we can't take that money," I said automatically. But I couldn't help being startled at the thought of leaving the house. Maybe it was that unsettled feeling, like there was still something bigger going on here that we hadn't figured out. Or maybe . . . My gaze wandered to Brynn, who was talking to Hal and George over near the door. She caught me looking and smiled, giving me a little wave.

I smiled back weakly. "Um, I don't know," I told Joe. "We thought we had this thing solved once before, remember? Maybe we should stick around—just in case."

Joe groaned. "You gotta be kidding," he said. "Aren't you feeling kind of—you know—*deprived* by now? No TV, no hot water . . ." Suddenly his voice trailed off and he grinned. He'd just followed my gaze. "Oh! I get it. Maybe you're not feeling so deprived after all."

My face went hot. Before I could answer, we both heard a shriek from just outside the room. A second later Georgina came running in. I hadn't even noticed she'd left, so she couldn't have been gone for long.

"I was just in that Deprivation Chamber thingy!" she blurted out. "You guys have got to see this!"

A moment later everyone was crowding into the small pod. Joe and I pushed our way to the front. When I saw the words scrawled on the chamber wall, my heart sank. In large, childish handwriting, someone had written: HOUSE OF DEATH.

"That wasn't there a few minutes ago," Olivia said, her voice shaking. "Gail and I were just in there!"

She was right. I realized I'd seen them emerging just before I'd spotted Mary outside. That meant there was no way Mary could have written it.

Joe leaned toward me. "Case open?" he murmured in my ear.

I nodded grimly. "Again."